THE
SANDSTORM
CONNECTION

by

Sheila & Ron Stewart

THE SANDSTORM CONNECTION

For everyone who reads our books, thank you. We hope they will encourage you to write your own book, or story, or song, or poem, or whatever you enjoy.

ONE

Lennie Barnes was just about the lowest form of life that Assistant Prosecuting Attorney, Lorraine Brensley had ever met in a court of law.

He was a drug dealer, a pusher, and a suspected murderer. He was also a sadistic psychopath who used phony friendships with less fortunate people on the streets to lure them into addiction or take the fall when he was caught in one of his criminal activities.

This was not the first time Lorraine had met Barnes and his high-priced lawyers in a courtroom. He had been charged or implicated in drug trafficking on more than one occasion. The previous time was when the Westland Police Department found drugs in the trunk of his car, along with a briefcase full of money and an assortment of weapons.

The trial didn't last long. The prosecutions' case was short lived when his driver, deciding that jail would be less painful than a bullet in the back of his head or a bomb under his car, accepted responsibility for the entire contraband. He took a plea, Lennie walked, and Lorraine's office was forced to wait for their next opportunity.

But this time was supposed to be different. This time the Westland Police Department had provided what appeared to be an air tight case to work with, including eye witnesses. Unfortunately the witnesses didn't show for the trial, and without their testimony to corroborate the evidence, the certainty of a conviction wasn't assured.

Lorraine studied the faces of the jurors as they returned to the courtroom from their deliberations, searching for the decision they would give. They did not return her gaze, but instead bowed their heads or looked in the direction of the defendant's table. It was not a good sign. When the jury foreman presented the judge with their verdict of not guilty on all counts, it was not entirely unexpected.

The judge thanked the jurors for their services and then dismissed them. When he had retired to his chambers, Lorraine was joined at her table by Private Investigator, Jennifer Brookbaine. Jennifer had never met Barnes, but she had seen his mug shot and heard his name, along with several other descriptions, several times as Lorraine was preparing her case for court.

"I don't think Lennie is inviting you to a church social," she remarked as Barnes glared triumphantly across the courtroom.

Lorraine looked in the direction of the drug dealer, the alleged drug dealer, with as much disdain as she could muster. "I wouldn't want to go to any church social that he was at anyway," she growled. "Not that you'll ever find him at one." A hint of a smile appeared on her face. "Now if you were to invite me to his hanging . . ."

Jennifer also smiled. "Don't worry. You'll hang him, eventually. Or he'll hang himself. Arrogant scum like him always make a mistake, sooner or later."

"I hope it's sooner," Lorraine replied. "I'm getting tired of watching him use the court house as a revolving door."

"Your office didn't give you a very strong case to work with," Jennifer reminded her.

Lorraine nodded in agreement. "I know. But it was all they had. We were counting on a couple of his so-called friends to testify against him, but they didn't show."

"Do you think that Lennie got to them and persuaded them to change their minds?"

"Probably. If they're still breathing. I was informed a few minutes ago that the Westland Police Department found a couple of bodies out in the desert that resembled them, or at least what was left of them."

"What would make them agree to testify in the first place? They must have known their lives wouldn't be worth much after Barnes found out."

"They probably knew, but did it anyway. He got them hooked on drugs, then raised the price so they couldn't afford them. When he cut off their supply and then tried to frame them for one of his deals to save his own neck, they were a little upset, so they turned him in and agreed to testify."

"Hell of a way to break an addiction. How come the police are having such a difficult time getting anything on him?"

"Because he uses other people to carry out most of his dirty work, while he stays in the background just far enough so that we know he has a finger in it but can't touch him. He also has the best legal defense that organized crime can buy. He's a front for somebody, but we don't know who. And we just saw what happens to anyone who offers to testify against him."

They watched as Barnes rose from a chair at his attorneys' table. Without as much as shaking their hands or acknowledging the defense they presented that had kept him out of prison, he headed out of the courtroom. On his way he swaggered past the table where Lorraine was seated. He sneered disdainfully at her. Lorraine could feel her own face twisting into a sneer, or at least as much of a sneer as the dignity of her position would allow.

He was followed by a woman in a yellow dress who had been sitting a few rows behind him. She was pretty, although she had obviously seen better days. Premature age lines had already begun to etch their way into her face and around her eyes, and her bleached blond hair had lost much of its luster. Lorraine had guessed her age at twenty-five or thirty, but she looked older. Life, or perhaps Lennie Barnes and his drugs had not been kind to her.

In contrast, Barnes' clothing could only be described as outlandish. Where most defendants attempted to dress as conservatively as possible in order to appear respectable to the judge and jury, he flaunted his attire. His blue jeans, multicolored cowboy boots, and gaudy silk shirts, although considered western attire, would have been more at home in the red light districts of a large metropolis than in the smaller southwestern city of Westland.

Barnes was also different in that life

appeared to have been too kind to him. Where his companion appeared frightened and subservient, he was cocky and dominant. He had never, even for a moment, shown any signs of concern in the courtroom. It was as if he knew the key witnesses against him wouldn't show and that the jury would find him not guilty, before the trial had even begun.

"I would have found him guilty from his appearance alone," Jennifer commented wryly as Barnes donned his cowboy hat and exited the courtroom.

"I would have too," Lorraine agreed. She glanced in the direction of the empty jurors box. "Unfortunately, I had these twelve other people in the courtroom who insisted on seeing some evidence."

"Who's the woman with him?" Jennifer asked. "His girl friend?"

"His sister, Linda," Lorraine answered. "I asked the police to check her out. She's single, and gives her address as an apartment building in the east end of the city, although they say she hardly ever goes there. The police said they couldn't find any history of drug abuse, but I'm not so sure. She looks like someone who might be using them."

"Maybe that's why she stays so close to her brother."

"Could be. Although she appears to be a little more respectable. At least she has a steady job. I looked into her background at the same time I checked out Lennie. She works in the accounting department at Wiley Electronics, a computer manufacturing company that is owned by a friend of ours. I know it isn't fair, but because of the crimes that her brother is involved in, and her closeness to him, it crossed my mind that she might be involved somehow in a problem they're having."

"What kind of problem?"

"Embezzlement. Apparently they've been losing a lot of money the past few months and Jim Wiley, the owner, can't figure out where it's going."

Jennifer's eyes lit up at the sound of embezzlement. "When will they know for sure?"

Lorraine smiled, guessing what her friend had in mind. "Jim has asked George's law firm to have a look around. So far he hasn't been able to turn up anything."

"Your husband, George?"

"The same. They've been friends since childhood, so George was happy to help in any way he could."

"Do you think there could be some kind of connection between the embezzlement at Wiley

Electronics, the coincidence that Linda Barnes works there, and her brother?"

"It had crossed my mind, and it could be worth looking into. I don't suppose you know a private investigator who might be interested in doing some snooping around."

"Are you kidding. You're darn right I'm interested. When do you think they'll know for sure?"

"Jim is flying in from his head office in New York this afternoon. George is picking him up at the airport. It will probably be a day or two before they get an idea of what's going on, or maybe even sooner. One of them will probably be giving you a call."

"What's this Jim Wiley like?"

"He's a nice guy, and very handsome. Do you know that you and he are about the same age. And you're both single. You never know where a relationship might lead. I can see romance, wedding bells, a house in the country, children, dogs . . ."

Jennifer screwed up her face. It wasn't the first time Lorraine had attempted match making. "Don't you think we should say hello first, and maybe go out on a date or something before you marry us. But on the other hand, if we did get married . . ."

Lorraine finished her thought. "Jim could

save a lot of money on investigation fees, and since he spends most of his time at his head office in New York or traveling around the world to his other companies, and you spend much of your time on stakeouts in Westland in the middle of the night, you wouldn't fight much."

"And with you working with me on this case of embezzlement, I'd have free legal advice."

"I can't work with you on this case. I already have a full time job trying to convict a low down murdering scumbag of a drug dealer named Lennie Barnes."

"Precisely. And that's why you'll want to work with me. I suspect there could be a connection somehow between Barnes, his sister, and Wiley Electronics, and if there is, between the two of us we're going to find it."

Lorraine couldn't help but nod in agreement. The thought of working with Jennifer on an investigation was something she always looked forward to, and even though her friend had not been formally asked yet, the more they talked, the more suspicious she was becoming that there could be a connection between Linda Barnes, her brother, and the missing money.

As they parted and Lorraine walked toward the prosecutor's office, she reflected on the frustrations she was experiencing in her quest to convict Lennie Barnes for the drug trafficking and other crimes she knew he was involved in, and the possibility of a connection through his sister to the embezzlement at Wiley Electronics.

Then both problems were pushed aside and replaced by memories of Jim Wiley and the years of friendship that she and her husband had shared with him.

A few miles away, George Brensley had just left his law office. As he turned onto the main thoroughfare that led toward Westland Airport, he thought about his wife and the frustrations she was experiencing with her trial.

Also on his mind were Jim Wiley and the problems his company was having with disappearing profits. Although he too was looking forward to seeing their friend, they were not meeting under the most positive circumstances.

Several car lengths behind, Lennie Barnes was also heading toward the airport to carry out an assignment for his superiors. The attorneys they provided for his defense did not come cheaply, and he was expected to pay for their time. He always did as he was told, because to do otherwise could bring an end to his criminal defense and freedom from prison, or like the two witnesses who were scheduled to testify at his trial, find himself out in the desert, full of bullets.

Lennie hated his bosses, and normally he resented being given orders by them, but this time would be an exception. This time he would take great pleasure in carrying out the assignment he had been given.

TWO

Jim Wiley watched the last remnants of sunset disappear into the western sky as the airplane banked and began its final approach into Westland Airport. Above, the February sky was still blue except for a few scattered clouds. Below, the streets were slowly being hidden by the early shadows of evening.

Jim didn't get back to Westland as often as he would like. Although he was born and raised in the desert city, most of his time was spent at Wiley Electronics International Sales Office in New York or traveling to the several manufacturing facilities his company owned throughout the world.

The Westland plant was the oldest part of the operation, having been opened by the Wiley family as a small welding and sheet metal shop in the mid nineteen hundreds. As the decades passed it grew and expanded into logistics and engineering that eventually included design and assembly of computers and other electronic systems.

Jim had managed the Westland plant until a few years earlier. When his father retired, he moved to New York to take over the international operations. He was about to plan another trip abroad when he received word that there were problems in Westland.

This trip would be partly business and partly pleasure. He would enjoy the pleasurable part, spending time with George and Lorraine Brensley, and seeing the many people he had worked with throughout the years. At the same time, he was reminded of the purpose of the visit. He was not looking forward to investigating the disappearing profits from his company or the possibility that someone he knew could be involved.

The plane touched down and taxied toward the terminal. Winter visitors who had flocked from the north and east to enjoy the warmth of the southwestern winter were talking excitedly to acquaintances who had arrived to meet them. Business people who had boarded the plane wearing more formal attire were now loosening buttons and carrying jackets.

"Jim."

He turned at the sound of George Brensley's voice. He had known George all his life and they were as much like brothers as they were friends. They also went to school together and had worked part time at Wiley Electronics while attending Westland University.

After graduating, George went on to Law School and married Lorraine, his boyhood sweetheart, while Jim stayed in the business full time. He had never married, and since he was now responsible for the international operations of Wiley Electronics, that was where most of his energy went.

He was tall, slim and handsome, and women were attracted to him. George and Lorraine couldn't help but notice. Sometimes in restaurants, they could see the additional attention given to him, or sense the slight suggestiveness in a waitress's voice as she led them to a table or brought them the check.

George was not quite as tall, and his hairline had begun to recede a little, which according to Lorraine just made him all the more handsome. And that was good enough for him. He didn't have the charisma his friend enjoyed, and that was also all right. After a long day at work he was quite happy to go home, put his feet up, and relax with his wife.

He gave Jim a hug. "You're looking well. I think chasing around the world must be good for you. You look better now than when Lorraine and I last saw you in New York. It must be all those women that keep you young. Probably all the exercise you get from running."

As he spoke, a flight attendant walked by. "Goodbye Mr. Wiley," she purred. "I hope I'll see you on another flight."

"You didn't," George exclaimed. "You must have. She looks too damned happy to have just served two hundred meals."

George liked to tease his friend about the attention he got from women. "Did you get her number? Are you still carrying that little black book you had in college? You must have to buy an extra seat just to carry it around."

Jim smiled. "I remember when you used to carry around a fairly thick little black book yourself."

"I remember. I was always trying to impress you, since you had so many girls chasing you all over the place. The truth is, I only had one name in it, Lorraine's."

"I knew that."

"How?"

"Lorraine showed it to me. You should know that you two don't have any secrets from each other. Sometimes I envy you, having only one name in your book, especially when it's her name. How's she doing? When I last spoke to her, she said she was having some difficulties with a case she was prosecuting. Some drug dealer?"

"A creep by the name of Lennie Barnes. She

has trouble mentioning his name without cussing. I talked to her just before she went to trial. A couple witnesses hadn't shown up and she was worried about how it would affect her case. If she loses, she's not going to be in a very good mood. It could show up in the meal she's planning for you tonight."

"What? Her cussing?"

"Her bad mood. Although from the way she sounded when I talked to her, I suppose there could be some cussing in there too."

"Maybe I could help. She could cuss her drug dealer, I could cuss our disappearing profits, and together we could come up with something really special for dinner."

"Not if you want me to eat it. Did you know that Barnes' sister works for you?"

"Really? What does she do?"

"A clerk of some kind in your purchasing and ordering department. From what I've heard, she's not like her brother. She appears to have a clean record. But you never know."

"I'm afraid to ask, but how is the rest of the company?"

"You're right. Don't ask."

"That bad, huh."

"Nah, unless you're expecting to show a profit or something. From what I've seen, the production line is building computers and getting them out the door all right, but you're still not making as much as your sales figures show you should be making. And with the business that has been coming in the past few months, you should be swimming in profits."

"Any idea where it's going?"

"Nope, but if I had to make a suggestion, I'd start asking questions in your regional manager's office. I met a brick wall there. He said he was looking into the problem and didn't need any help from me."

"Carl Rogers?"

"I'm afraid so."

"Carl's a good man. A little stubborn at times, that's all."

"I know he's a good man, but he's being more than just a little stubborn. I know he was a friend of your father, and you owe him a lot, but I think he's over his head in the manager's position. He just doesn't seem interested in finding out where the money is going. I'm not sure he even believes money is missing."

Jim understood. "I trust Carl, and I'm sure he wouldn't steal from the company, but I also know what you mean about his interest in the manager's position. He was much happier when he was in sales and marketing, before he took over the job. Have you talked to anyone else?"

"I spent some time in manufacturing and shipping. I also asked a few questions in the area where Linda Barnes works. Maybe it wasn't fair to her, but her brother's reputation influenced me. I didn't see anything out of the ordinary."

"Anywhere else?"

"No. I didn't think I should go too far over Carl's head, or behind his back, or wherever I'd be going. And even if I did, I'm not sure what I'd be looking for. Crooks, good at manipulating numbers, probably have a thousand ways to add up figures and make them equal anything they want. Anyway, I thought that digging further into the company's accounting procedures and seeing what else someone might be hiding in the books, would be a job best left to you."

Jim nodded in agreement. Examining the company's accounting procedures would be a job best left to him. Also best, although more uncomfortable, would be meeting with Carl Rogers, asking what he knew about the missing profits, and seeking his help in finding the people responsible.

In spite of Carl's occasional stubbornness, for many years he had worked hard to make the company successful, and was a much appreciated friend of Jim's father. He was also promised the regional manager's position if it became available, and although Jim had some reservations, he also agreed that the promotion was earned. So when he moved to New York to take over the company's international operations, he carried out his father's wishes and gave Carl the job.

"Maybe we should look into having someone carry out some investigations in the plant," he suggested.

"Already have," George replied. "We have a friend who's a private investigator, and Lorraine is going to ask if she's interested."

"Did you say, she, like a female private investigator?"

"Yes. She's darned good at it too. And also very beautiful. Lorraine said that you and she would make a . . ."

"A what? Are you and Lorraine trying to set me up again?"

"No, no, of course not. At least I'm not. Lorraine, well you know how Lorraine is. Ever since I mentioned that I might have an investigation for Jennifer to carry out, she's been looking forward to the two of you getting together."

"Then I'll just have to meet this beautiful private investigator," Jim replied. "When can we make an appointment?"

"Probably sooner than you think, if your problems become as difficult to find as they appear."

George led the way out of the arrivals area and toward the elevators that led to the parking garage. As they waited, the flight attendant who had spoken to them a few minutes earlier waved and repeated her promise to see Jim Wiley again.

"Where do you keep it?" George asked.

"What?"

"The stuff that attracts them to you."

"You have the same stuff," Jim snapped back. "You just choose to keep yours at home. And if I had a great wife like Lorraine, I'd be staying at home too."

George's grin turned mischievous. "One of these days . . . Who knows, maybe Lorraine's friend is the one. Maybe Jennifer could settle you down."

They stepped out of the elevator and headed across the parking garage toward George's Buick. He was about to open the trunk to put in a suitcase when Jim put up his hand.

"Hold it George," he said. "Don't open the trunk, or anything else, not yet. And be careful. Don't move anything."

"What? Why not? What are you looking for?" George stood by in bewilderment as his friend checked the undercarriage of the car, then slowly walked around, examining it as he moved.

Jim stopped at the front bumper, inspected the hood which was slightly ajar, then carefully slid his hand in and moved the secondary emergency latch. He slowly lifted the hood, gazed at the engine for a few seconds, then motioned for George to join him.

"Take a look," he said. "But don't touch anything."

George carefully peered over the front of the car and examined the engine compartment, searching for whatever it was that Jim had wanted him to see. Everything appeared to be where it should be.

Everything, except the bundle of dynamite that had been wedged behind the motor.

THREE

The bomb in George Brensley's Buick consisted of six sticks of dynamite held together with electrical tape. It had been wedged between the motor and the fire wall so that most of the explosion would travel back into the passenger compartment.

Wiring ran from a detonator inserted into the dynamite, to a battery power supply that would provide necessary voltage to set it off. Another set of wires ran to a printed circuit board on which a digital timer and an activation switch were fastened.

The activation switch served as the electrical connection. It resembled a leveling device, and as long as its contacts stayed apart, it would not activate. But if it was tilted, or jarred enough to move the contacts from the safe end of the tube it was encased in, to the other end where the contacts met, it would start the timer.

George continued to stare at the bomb, trying to determine how much time they would have after the switch was triggered, the timer began its countdown, and the dynamite went off. There was no way to tell.

Everything in his body was telling him to run, except his feet which had suddenly deserted him. His legs joined them in the mutiny and he leaned against an automobile behind him for support. He shuddered at the thought of what could have happened if Jim Wiley had not discovered the bomb and prevented him from starting and moving his car.

"How the hell did you know that was in there?" he exclaimed when he finally caught his breath. "I don't care how you knew, I'm just glad you did."

He took another deep breath and looked inquisitively at his friend. "How the hell did you know?"

"I didn't," Jim replied. "Not for sure. But I saw a woman hurrying away from your car as we were approaching, and she was acting suspiciously. She kept looking back as if she knew us, then she began to run. She headed that way, toward the other side of the parking garage."

He had already begun to hurry in the direction where he had last seen the woman he suspected of planting the bomb. George ran to catch up with him. "But that's not enough to make you suspect a bomb."

"It is when it's happened before. Somebody

blew themselves up in a parking garage near our office in New York. The police said they were carrying a bomb that's activated by motion, maybe the same as this one. Anyway, they must have moved it because it went off before they were able to install it. Whoever planted this bomb appears to have been a little more competent. They attached a timer to give themselves an opportunity to get away if they screwed up."

"Do you think the bomb in New York was meant for your car?"

"I didn't, until now."

"Why didn't you tell me about it?"

"I wasn't certain. And I didn't want to worry you, and Lorraine. If it will make you feel better, you can start worrying now."

"I will. I'm glad you found the bomb, but what made you check under the hood?"

"It was slightly ajar, so I decided to have a look before you got into your car and started it. I opened the hood the rest of the way, inspected the motor, and there it was."

A squeal of tires from the other side of the parking garage interrupted their conversation. They heard the squeals again, then a car's roof came into view and a dark grey Mercedes Benz raced out of an aisle, swung around a row of automobiles, and accelerated toward them.

They attempted to get a look at the occupants through the tinted windshield, but under the faint glow from the lights in the parking garage, it was impossible to make them out.

The driver suddenly swerved in an attempt to run them over, and in the moment it took for them to leap for cover, the automobile had screeched around another corner, past the aisle where George's Buick was parked, and disappeared down a ramp. A moment later, they heard wood splintering as the Mercedes crashed through the flimsy barrier at the exit. They caught sight of it once more as it raced along the pavement that led out of the airport, and then it was gone.

Jim was writing as much as he could remember from the short time they had seen the vehicle, when they heard another squeal of tires from the same direction the Mercedes had appeared.

A moment later a small red convertible sped toward them and they were forced to jump for cover once again. The car raced by, swerved between the rows of automobiles, and skidded into a parking space with its bumper approaching the front of the Buick.

It was only a glancing blow, but the sound of the two cars colliding caused them to run toward the driver to warn him about the bomb.

They didn't need to. The young man who was driving had already shut off the ignition, leaped over the convertible's door, and was running toward the terminal elevator.

Jim grabbed his arm as he passed and pulled him behind the fender of a pickup truck. The young man had just begun to demand an explanation when the timing device attached to the dynamite did its job. For five seconds it was very quiet, then the Buick was rocked with an explosion.

A ball of red and yellow flame blasted the hood off its hinges and it skyrocketed upwards, hitting the ceiling of the garage. Still burning, it landed on a nearby automobile. At the same instant, the doors blew open, the windows shattered, and smoke and fire burst from the interior.

At the first sound of the explosion the driver had pressed himself against the truck beside the two men, then he cautiously raised his head and peered over a fender. Fascinated, he stared at the fire as it spread toward the rear of the Buick. He ducked again when the gas tank exploded, blew the trunk lid open, and engulfed the surrounding area in flames.

When the eruptions finally ceased, he slowly stood up and stared at the burning remains of the Buick, his convertible, and the other vehicles that were caught in the blast. As pieces of debris drifted toward him, his arms opened wide in astonishment.

"Wow!" he exclaimed in a voice that appeared to be filled with awe more than it was fear. "What have you got there?"

His attention moved to his convertible. "Hey, look at what happened to my car. I just had that painted."

George eyed him suspiciously. "It was a bomb. You set it off when you ran into my car."

"What were you doing with a bomb in your car?" The driver's forehead furrowed into suspicions of his own. "Oh no you don't. You're not going to pin this on me. I hardly touched it. Maybe your gas was too rich, maybe you need a tune-up. Maybe you need to stop carrying explosives in your car."

George's voice took on a more accusatory tone. "I told you, it was a bomb. Somebody put it there, and we're going to find out who it was."

The driver and George eyed each other suspiciously. He was a young man, in his early twenties, with wavy hair that looked like it had taken him most of the day to comb. He had shown no fear when the bomb went off and still didn't show any.

"Somebody must really hate you," he said. His gaze returned to the still burning Buick. "A lot. What are you? Gangsters? Politicians? Lawyers . . . ?"

When there was no acknowledgment of an occupation, the young man's face changed into a smile and the enjoyment of twisting an imaginary knife into George's suspicions.

"Late with alimony payments . . . ?"

Out of guesses, he wavered back and forth as if searching for a gun under George's neatly tailored suit. Seeing no bumps there, he stared curiously at the two men to confirm he wasn't in any danger himself. "And you're not gangsters."

When they didn't respond, he continued. "That must have been a good size bomb, five, maybe six sticks of dynamite."

"How did you know there were six sticks of dynamite in the bomb?"

The young man hesitated, enjoying the moment. Then he spread his arms in a sweeping gesture that took in most of the crime scene. "We wouldn't be standing here if it was military explosives. We'd be spread around the parking garage."

George gave him another distrusting stare. "How do you know so much about explosives?"

"Construction. I worked for my father's

construction company last summer. They sometimes used dynamite to clear away little things that got in the way, such as boulders, hills, mountains . . ."

"Is that what you did? Blow up boulders, and hills, and mountains?"

"Sort of. I blew up some of my father's construction equipment."

George looked toward the remains of where the young man's car used to be. "What did you do? Run into them?"

"No."

"What?"

"I sat, accidentally sat, on a switch they were using for detonation, before they had a chance to clear the area of equipment. The explosion and following fire destroyed a pickup truck, a gravel truck, a bulldozer, a backhoe, and a few other of my father's prized possessions that were still parked near the blasting area."

"So you know a lot about dynamite and bombs."

The young man dismissed the insinuation in George's question. "Just dynamite, enough to know what six sticks of it can do. You guys were lucky, you know."

"Yeah, yeah, we know."

"No, I mean you were lucky your car blew up."

"What!"

"You're lucky it was blown up. When I blew up . . . accidentally blew up . . . my father's construction equipment, there was just enough left for the occupational safety organization that looks after such things to take it away. They've had them locked in an impound lot ever since, trying to figure out what happened."

"Didn't you tell them?"

"I couldn't."

"Why not?"

"They forgot to ask me."

"So how does that make us lucky?"

"Because the police will be doing the same thing with your car and my convertible. They'll take them to the crime lab and try to figure out what happened to what's left of them, which of course, we already know. But here's the lucky part. Since there is nothing left of them, we can take our insurance money and go buy ourselves new cars."

"I don't suppose you still work for your father?"

"No. He was a little upset when a tailgate from the pickup truck went through the roof of his Cadillac. Perhaps if he hadn't been sitting in it . . ."

The young man spread his arms to indicate

a distance of three or four feet. "I missed my inheritance by this much."

He looked again at the burning wreckage and then at the two men. "Anything else you need to know about explosives . . . ?"

Assuming they didn't, he turned and began walking away.

"I'll be seeing you."

"Hold it right there," George demanded. "I want to know why you came along at the same time as the people who put the bomb in my car and then tried to run over us, why you also tried to run over us, and why you hit my car and set off the bomb, I think there's a connection somehow between you and the people in the Mercedes, and I'm going to find out what it is."

The young man stopped. "There is no connection, I didn't try to run over you, I just touched the bumper, and how was I to know you keep bombs in your car. Besides, you were standing in the middle of the aisle, and I was late for work. And if I don't get in there, I won't have any work to go to because they'll fire me."

He scanned the wreckage. "Besides, I think you might have a difficult time proving *anything* ran into your car. I don't see any scratches."

"Wait," George demanded again. "What about your car?"

The young man looked at the smoldering wreckage of what was once his convertible. "You can have it. I have another one at home. My father gave it to me . . . before I destroyed his Cadillac. It's very similar to this one, except it hasn't been blown up yet."

He turned again, stopping only long enough to pick up an identifying ornament that had blown off the Buick, then continued his walk toward the terminal.

"Come back here," George ordered.

"Sorry," he said. "I'm late. I'll be inside if you need me."

The young man quickly made his way through a crowd which had begun to form. George attempted to follow but was stopped by an airport traffic patrolman.

"What happened here?" the officer exclaimed when he saw the wreckage.

"Somebody planted a bomb in my car."

"A what?"

"A bomb."

"Is anybody hurt?"

"No."

"Any witnesses?"

"Just us."

George pointed to the driver of the

convertible, who had almost reached the terminal elevator. "And that man. He hit my car and set off the bomb."

"He isn't going anywhere," the patrolman responded as he pulled a cell phone from a holster on his belt. "He works on the arrivals level. I'll call this in, if someone else hasn't already, and then I'll tell him to get his ass back up here."

While the officer made his calls, George reached into a pocket for his own cell phone to call Lorraine and let her know what had taken place. She was not in her office. Not wanting to cause her any more worry than necessary until they met, his description of the devastation went something like . . .

"I picked up Jim, having a little problem with the Buick, something in the motor, not running at present. Will pick up a rental car. Will tell you everything that happened when we get there. Jim says hello. Love you."

To George, the message sounded less worrisome than, "Bomb in car. Blew up and took a few other cars with it. Lucky to be alive. We might have seen one, possibly two of the people who did it, but they got away. Waiting for police to arrive. Jim says it's okay to worry."

As he disconnected, he looked once again at

the burned out remains of his Buick, the young man's convertible, and the burning vehicles that surrounded them, then turned to Jim Wiley.

"I think," he said, "we could be just a tad late getting home."

Jim joined him in viewing the remains. "I think," he replied, "we could be more than just a tad late."

FOUR

Lieutenant Raymond Lindsay had served in the Westland Police Department for more years than he could be bothered remembering. He was eligible for retirement but opted to stay on the force. First, he was good at his job, second, he enjoyed doing it, and third, he had no idea how he would occupy himself if he did retire.

His thick silver-gray hair lay like a mop on his head and the tips of a similarly colored mustache stretched outward over his slightly puffed cheeks. He was in fairly good shape, although middle age spread was beginning to show above his belt. All in all, he had the weathered appearance of a grumpy old timer who had seen just about everything there was to see in crime.

He examined the charred remains of the Buick, along with what was left of the convertible and other cars around it, in a way that suggested the bomb blast wasn't the first he had seen. Then with a mixture of curiosity and suspicion he peered over his reading glasses at Jim Wiley and George Brensley.

"You two involved with organized crime of some kind?"

George spoke defensively. "Noooo . . ."

"Do you know anyone in organized crime?"

"Noooo . . ."

"Who do you think did this?"

"We don't know."

"It sure looks like the work of organized crime."

Jim stepped in. "Like George said, we don't know anyone in organized crime. We saw a woman, who appeared to be doing something to George's car, hurry away when she saw us approach. Then we discovered a bundle of dynamite behind the motor, attached to some kind of detonator. We gave chase but before we could catch her, someone in a Mercedes Benz, probably with her in it, tried to run us down as they raced out of the parking garage."

George pointed to what was left of the red convertible. "And then the driver of that car ran into my car and set off the bomb. He said it was an accident, but I'm not completely convinced. He came along at the same time as the Mercedes. He also almost ran over us, he knew a lot about dynamite, and he had experience in setting off explosives."

"What kind of experience?"

George searched for words to describe the

driver's encounter with explosives. Not completely finding them, he finally replied, "According to him, he sat on a switch and blew up his father's construction company."

There was no hesitation from Lindsay. "That should be enough to take care of a little job like this."

The lieutenant looked into the convertible as though expecting to see the smoldering remains of a mangled corpse. Not seeing anyone there, he looked around the parking garage for body pieces. As a last resort, he stared at the ceiling. Seeing nothing sticking to it, he returned to his questioning.

"What happened to the driver of the convertible?"

"He got out of his car before the explosion," Jim explained. "We couldn't keep him here. According to the security officer over there, he works inside the terminal. Another officer is apparently keeping an eye on him, making sure he doesn't leave."

Lindsay began scribbling notes. "I'll get to the security officer and the driver of the convertible soon enough, after I find out everything you two know about it. The woman you saw running away from your car, what did she look like?"

"It was difficult to tell," Jim said. "We were

quite a distance from her, and she was facing the other direction."

"Can you describe her?"

"I can't tell you much. I didn't get a look at her face. She was probably five feet, maybe taller. Her hair was blonde, about shoulder length, and she wore a yellow dress."

"What can you tell me about the Mercedes she was in?"

Jim handed him the paper with the information he had written. "Large, like a limo, gray in color. We got the licence plate number. The windows were tinted, so we couldn't tell if she was driving or someone else was."

Lindsay quickly examined the information and tucked the paper into his notes. "It will probably have a new paint job and license plates by the time we see it again. But I'll call it in anyway. Who knows, if they can screw up something as simple as blowing up a car, maybe they'll forget."

"You married?" he asked Jim.

"No."

"Girlfriends?"

"Not at present."

"Anybody in your past who wouldn't mind seeing you spread around a parking garage? Ex-wife, ex-girlfriend, maybe an old flame with a long memory, blond, five feet or so tall, wears a yellow dress, drives a Mercedes, likes to blow up things."

Jim saw the direction the questions were going. "How about two men in a New York parking garage, carrying a bomb, near my company headquarters, blew themselves up before they could plant it."

"Huh . . . Were you the target? Was the target your car?"

"I don't know, and I'm glad I didn't have to find out. They never made it to whatever was their target."

"But you must think there could be a connection to this bombing?"

"I don't know that either. I just know the bomb in New York was close enough to my business, and made me nervous enough to check George's car when I saw the woman running away from it."

"Did you just fly in from New York?"

"Yes."

"Do you go to other countries?"

"A few."

"And your business is . . . ?"

Jim held out a business card. "Wiley Electronics. We have an electrical engineering and computer manufacturing company on the north side of town."

The lieutenant examined the card and nodded his recognition of the facility. "I'll call the New York Police and see what they've learned about the bombing there. Anybody know you were coming here today?"

"Just George, a couple people in my office, and Carl Rogers, our district manager here in Westland. I suppose he could have told someone I was coming or someone could have overheard his conversation with me. I didn't tell him the purpose of the visit, or let him know exactly when I was coming."

Lindsay turned to George. "Can you think of any reason why someone would want to see you strewn around a parking garage?"

"Why are you asking me?"

"It was your car."

"Oh . . . ? No. I was doing some investigating at Jim's company, about some missing money, but I didn't get the impression that anybody was feeling threatened."

"You never know. Sometimes we don't find out these things . . ." The lieutenant cocked a thumb and tilted his head in the direction of the burned out remains of George's Buick. "Until . . ."

He accepted another business card. It did not receive the recognition that Wiley Electronics' card had received. "You must have met quite a few people in your line of work who aren't happy. Anybody know you were coming to the airport?"

"No. I told my secretary I was leaving, but I don't think I mentioned I was coming here."

"Did you notice anybody following you?"

"Hell, no. I don't look for people following me. But I will now."

"You got a girlfriend?"

"I'm married."

"You got a girlfriend?" Lindsay repeated.

Like Jim, George knew where the questions were going. He had heard them many times in court when a suspect's lawyer was trying to divert fault away from a client.

"No. My wife won't let me have one."

He turned his attention to Jim again. "The investigation in your company? Tell me about it."

"We're still searching for the source," Jim replied. "A lot of money has disappeared and we don't know where. The only connection George might have uncovered is a lady in the purchasing department. She appears innocent enough, but she has a brother in the drug business. He's appearing in court today."

"The Lennie Barnes case?" Lindsay asked.

"Yes. Do you know Lennie Barnes?"

"I know of him. We think organized crime

is footing the bill for his defense, and maybe disposing of two witnesses who were found out in the desert, that were scheduled to testify."

"Dead?" George asked.

Lindsay nodded. "The woman you saw in purchasing? What did this woman look like?"

"Fairly attractive, blond. Other than that, I didn't pay too much attention to her."

"Anything else?"

"No . . . Oh . . ."

"Oh . . .?"

"She was wearing a yellow dress."

Lindsay motioned to Jim with a thumb. "Like the one he described?"

"I suppose."

"Do either of you see some kind of connection here?"

"I do now," George said.

"Do you have her address?"

"I can get it for you," Jim said, "or she should be at work in the morning."

"Unless she skips town or is sleeping out in the desert with the two witnesses, for screwing up the bombing. I'll get information on her from headquarters, and If I don't find her, I'll visit your company in the morning to see if she shows up."

"Are you saying you think Linda Barnes could be responsible for this?" George asked.

"I do, I do" Lindsay answered. "But not by herself. I suppose it could be as simple as one lady being disappointed with something one of you did to her. But a bomb is not the way a proper lady usually goes about such things, might break a nail or something. A proper lady would prefer to put something in your cocktail or have her new boyfriend take care of you."

"Or," he said to Jim, "and you might recognize this one. She could have decided to get a job with your company and take you for every cent she can get out of you."

"Oh."

"Maybe you dated her a long time ago. Maybe kindergarten or something. Scorned women can have pretty long memories."

"I wasn't dating in kindergarten," Jim snapped back. "I was riding my bicycle around the school yard."

"Maybe you ran over her," George offered.

George and the lieutenant watched as past romances passed through Jim's mind. Finally he shook his head. "Sorry," he replied. "I still don't remember her."

"Try this, then," Lindsay said. "Insert a brother into the mix, who is knee deep in drugs and other criminal activities. Add an, as yet, unknown crime family that keeps him out of jail and gets rid of witnesses out in the desert. Throw in your botched bombing in New York, which appears to me to be very similar to this bombing, connect the bombing there to the bombing here, or the other way around, it doesn't matter, and we have something a little bigger."

He pointed a thumb at George. "I think that one of you, possibly with his investigation, could have gotten too close to something a lot more substantial, and whoever is behind it has decided to get rid of one, or my guess, both of you."

"Like what?"

"You name it. Drugs, smuggling, money laundering. An international company like yours would be perfect for a crime syndicate's operation."

"What about just plain old stealing?" George asked.

"Not enough," Lindsay replied. "Not if organized crime is involved. You keep looking for your money. I'm going to be looking at the larger picture, and maybe we can put the two of them together."

"In Westland?" Jim exclaimed.

"In Westland," Lindsay replied.

He flipped a page in his note pad and continued to scribble information. After asking more questions about the woman and the bombing, and apparently satisfied for the moment that they had given him everything they knew, he told them to remain where they were in case he needed more information. Then he turned and walked toward the smoldering wreckage where a forensics team was carefully picking up one piece of the Buick and then another, searching for evidence.

Ignoring his demand not to move, the two men followed.

A few minutes later Lindsay shifted his gaze to the convertible that had run into it and set off the bomb. Appearing to pay more attention to it than he had the Buick, he checked the information in his note pad, flipped another page, and made more notes.

"Interesting," he said out loud to himself.

"Do you think you found something?" George asked.

"I do," Lindsay replied. "I think I found a connection between the driver of the red convertible and the lady in the yellow dress."

FIVE

Darkness had set in and what was left of the short evening rush hour in Westland had thinned to a few drivers by the time Jennifer Brookbaine arrived to give Lorraine a ride home and to show off the sports car she had just purchased.

They exited through a side door and walked to the parking lot. "New?" Lorraine asked as she slid into the low profile vehicle and buckled her seat belt.

"Used," Jennifer replied. "And it really hugs the road." She turned the ignition, listened to the rumble of the high horsepower motor, then peeled onto the street. "Ten years old, but low mileage. The salesman said it was a Cream Puff."

"Cream Puff?"

"Cream Puff. Well cared for. The owner was one of their long time steady customers who gave it regular service. I bought it from a dealer a few blocks from here. It will make a good stakeout car for some of the places where I have to leave it parked. Thieves will be less apt to steal it once they see it's not new. What do you think?"

"I think my ass just touched a speed bump," Lorraine said as she applied imaginary brakes from the passenger's seat. "I can see what you mean about hugging the road. My question is, do car thieves actually care if a sports car is new or used. A better question might be, do car thieves even know if a sports car is new or used?"

"Okay, I bought it because it looks nice, I enjoy driving it, and if I ever make any money, I can claim it on my income tax. Leave me alone."

"Are you not making money?"

"Of course I am, but when people insist on paying cash, it's sometimes difficult to remember it all."

"You do know that I am a Prosecuting Attorney for the City of Westland."

"Oh. Forget everything I just said. Am I going to meet this Jim Wiley person at your place tonight? Is he still in need of a private investigator?" A crooked smile formed on Jennifer's face. "Does he pay cash?"

"From what George tells me, he doesn't have a lot of cash left, thanks to the embezzlement that's been going on in his company, but maybe if you help him find it he'll give you some."

"I thought he was rich."

"He was, but now, with the missing money, I think he's down to his last five-hundred million dollars or so."

"That's promising. You did say he was handsome?"

"Very. And that's why I think you and he would make such a great couple. But first we'll have to see if he even wants you."

"Thanks."

Jennifer eased up on the accelerator until they left the streets of downtown Westland and merged onto the freeway that led to the outskirts of town. A few miles later, she turned onto a less-traveled road that gently sloped upwards into the foothills and the Brensleys' home. Most of the land on either side was vacant or in the process of being developed, and construction crews that had been working were closed down for the day.

There were no other vehicles on the road, although one had turned off the freeway at the same exit they had. Jennifer watched its headlights in her rear view mirror. When she slowed down to give it an opportunity to pass, the driver also slowed down and kept pace a few hundred feet behind. She increased her speed, only to have it keep pace again.

"I don't mean to alarm you," she said, "but I think a car might be following us. I didn't spot them on the freeway, but someone is there now."

"I see them," Lorraine answered. "You don't suppose Lennie Barnes . . . ?"

"I wouldn't be surprised. I don't think you're his favorite attorney right now. Do you have a gun with you?"

Lorraine reached into her handbag and lifted out the small twenty-two-caliber-five-shot pistol she had carried since receiving threats from some, not so happy, criminals she convicted or helped convict.

Jennifer looked at the tiny gun. "And what are you going to do with that? Throw your bullets at them?"

"I have a bigger one at home if you would like me to go and get it. What would you suggest?"

"Perhaps something a little bigger." Jennifer reached into her handbag and pulled out the snub-nosed thirty-eight revolver she always carried. "Maybe the bullets from this will reach them."

Lorraine accepted the thirty-eight, checked the safety, and rested it on the seat beside her. "If I need it. I thought you were going to get a more modern gun."

"I was," Jennifer replied, "but I decided I like this one better. It doesn't spit out empty shell casings for the police to count, and I get to put them in my handbag and take them home where I know they won't get into any more trouble."

"You do realize that I'm a . . ."

"Yeah, yeah, I know. A Prosecuting Attorney for the City of Westland. In the meantime, let's see what this baby will do."

Jennifer shoved the accelerator to the floor. The car responded, but not with the power she had expected. At the same time a puff of bluish-grey smoke blew out from beneath the chassis. Just as quickly, the pursuing vehicle caught up and once again kept pace a few car lengths behind.

"I thought your Cream Puff was supposed to be powerful," Lorraine said, "and what's the smoke I see?"

"I don't know," Jennifer answered, "and I'm not about to stop to find out. Maybe they're just visiting the area, and looking for a place to pass."

She stepped on the accelerator again. More blue smoke blustered out from under the rear end and the other car continued to keep pace.

Lorraine peered through the oil filled mist that was drifting behind, partially hiding the following car's headlights. "Or a good place for an ambush."

Their questions were answered when a bullet careened off the roof. Then a group of bullets from a semiautomatic weapon thudded into the back of the car. The next group blew out the rear window.

As Jennifer swerved, Lorraine returned fire with her smaller pistol through the hole where the window had once been, taking aim at the windshield and the driver. She didn't see any effect. She did the same with Jennifer's thirty-eight. If any of the bullets found their mark, she had no way of knowing. The one thing she did know was that the windshield was still there, the driver was still in control, and the car was about to overtake them.

"They're coming up beside us!" she called out in a voice that was struggling to remain calm but had a touch of panic attached.

"Good." Jennifer's respond was cooler than expected.

"You got a plan?" Lorraine asked.

"Sort of. Duck."

Lorraine sank into the seat as far as she could. "That's your plan??!! Duck??!!"

Jennifer did the same. "At the moment, it's the only plan I can think of." A moment later, she slammed on the brakes.

A flash of fire erupted from a semiautomatic pistol as a Mercedes Benz sped past. Bullets exploded through the side window over Jennifer's head, then exploded again as they blew out the other side window above Lorraine. Additional bullets missed the car and tore into the darkness of the night as it passed.

Lorraine peered over the dash as the Mercedes pulled back in front of them. "Are you all right?" she gasped.

Jennifer stepped on the gas and took off after the other car. "I'm all right, but they're not. The sons of bitches just made me mad."

The Mercedes wasn't making an effort to get away. The driver veered from side to side to give the passenger a clear shot and gunfire continued to pour in bursts from the automatic pistol.

Jennifer zigzagged back and forth, trying to stay directly behind and out of range. Lorraine remained crouched behind the dash as she returned fire through the hole where the side window had shattered and disappeared.

"Hold on to your britches."

Jennifer slammed into, and under, the back of the Mercedes and pushed it, or attempted to push it, along the winding road. "At least they're going to know they've been in a fight," she yelled at the car ahead.

Lorraine and the Cream Puff were not as

confident. With each push, the engine's coughs grew longer and louder, and the blue smoke became thicker and darker. At the same time, the metal in the front end began screaming and struggling under the weight of the heavier vehicle that was now sitting on its hood.

Jennifer slammed into the Mercedes one more time, then hit the brakes and jerked the steering wheel hard to the left. As her car skidded sideways to a stop on the narrow pavement, the other vehicle flew off the road and disappeared.

Lorraine searched the darkness of the desert to see where it had gone. Jennifer did the same as she backed up to where the Mercedes had become airborne. Off in the distance it sat motionless in the swirls of dust that had been kicked up when it landed.

Through the haze they could make out the faint outline of a yellow dress as the driver's door opened and closed. A woman quickly walked around to the passenger's side and climbed back in. Lorraine strained to see her through the billowing dust.

"Lennie Barnes' sister!!??"

"I don't know," Jennifer replied. "It could be. I couldn't make her out in the dust. There's no sign of Lennie, but he could be the new driver."

"Whoever they are, they aren't familiar with this area, or they would have known about that turn. Too bad the sons of bitches aren't upside down under their car."

The Mercedes began to move. Sand and gravel were kicked up from beneath the tires as the driver skidded back and forth through the loose soil in search of a way back to the highway.

"I think we'd better get the hell out of here," Lorraine said as they stared at the slowly circling headlights. "We can tangle with them later when we reach home and get a little more firepower, and the odds are a little more even."

In agreement, Jennifer stepped on the accelerator. A mixture of steam and oil continued to hiss from the worn out engine and from where bullets had found their marks. The old car gave what energy it had left and the tires offered a feeble chirp on the pavement as they slowly made their escape.

"Would you like some good news or some bad news?" She offered as the lights of the Brensleys' residence appeared in the distance.

"What's the good news?"

"I can see your house."

"And the bad news?"

"We're not going to make it. The temperature gauge is out of sight, the check oil light has been on for the past two miles, and the engine is sputtering like we're out of fuel. Do you know somewhere we can hide?"

Lorraine examined their surroundings, then pointed to a driveway.

"Turn in there."

Jennifer strained to see faint lights through the darkness. "What's in there?"

"A church."

"A church? What are we going to do with a church? Pray?"

"No, silly. The church choir meets here every week at this time. If we're lucky, they'll still be here."

"And what are they going to do? Help us pray?"

Jennifer swung what was left of her Cream Puff into the driveway. Ahead, they could see the lights of a small country church. To Lorraine, its steeple was a welcome beacon, and hopefully the activity beyond the stained glass windows meant people and safety.

To Jennifer, not so much. She brought the car to a stop in an empty space in the middle of the lot, cut the motor, and turned off the lights. Singing could be heard coming from the building, then it stopped and people began to exit.

"Hello Lorraine."

Reverend Baldwin was peering in through a hole in what used to be a side window. Some other church members were looking in through the opening where the rear window was once located.

"Good evening Reverend," Lorraine replied with a weak smile.

Baldwin ran his fingers over indentations and holes that bullets had made in a fender, then scrutinized the rest of the car. "Do you need some help. Are you in some kind of trouble?"

"A little. Some people in a Mercedes Benz took some shots at us."

"Are they still around?"

As he spoke, the headlights of an automobile coming from the direction where the Mercedes went off the road slowed down at the end of the driveway, and then sped up again. It moved a quarter mile past until its brake lights came on. It slowed down and turned around.

"I'm afraid so," Lorraine replied as the car came to a stop at the church entrance and slowly began to enter. "Whoever is in that car did the shooting."

"I'll call the police and let them know what happened," the reverend said with a reassuring smile, "and maybe we can do something until they get here."

He turned away and talked to the other church members who were beginning to gather around Jennifer's bullet-riddled car. They spread out to their respective cars and pickup trucks. When they returned, they were carrying an assortment of weapons.

"Ranchers," Lorraine explained to Jennifer. "Many members of the congregation own ranches and carry a gun in their vehicles in case they run into pests that bother their livestock, and I suppose the occasional two-legged pest, such as our friends in the Mercedes."

"Even the choir?"

"Even the choir."

"The police have been notified," Baldwin informed them. "In the meantime we can look after you."

"We don't want to get you involved," Lorraine said to the reverend. "There could be gunfire. If you could perhaps lend us a couple weapons . . ."

"Don't mention it," Baldwin answered. "And don't worry about us getting involved. We're happy to help out." He held his rifle in the air so that there was no mistaking what he was holding. The rest of the congregation followed suit.

The Mercedes sat at the end of the driveway

while its occupants considered the situation. Apparently deciding that a shootout with an armed church congregation was not in their best interests, the driver backed onto the road and sped off into the night.

As they watched the tail lights fade out of sight, Lorraine reached inside her purse for her cell phone. "I'd better call George," she said, "and let him know we'll be a little late getting home for dinner."

Not wanting to cause him any worry, her message went something like, "Other than your Buick stalling, glad you're having a good day. Jennifer's car is having a similar problem. Not running at present. We are at Reverend Baldwin's church. Congregation is helping. Not sure we can get it going. Might have to have it towed. Will be just a tad late getting home. Will fill you in when we get there. Love you. Say hello to Jim."

To Lorraine it sounded less worrisome than, "Ambushed on highway. Jennifer's car shot full of holes. Almost got killed. We think it might have been Lennie Barnes and his sister. Fortunately, Reverend Baldwin's choir had enough guns to save our lives. See you in a little while. Lucky to be alive. Don't worry. Love you both."

Police sirens and lights could already be

heard and seen approaching as she returned her attention to Jennifer, the bullet riddled, oil spewing, no longer coughing and sputtering Cream Puff, and Reverend Baldwin.

Jennifer stared longingly at her mortally wounded transportation.

"I wonder," she said, "who the Westland Police Department will be sending out to sort through this mess."

A few miles away, on the arrivals level in the Westland Airport, a cell phone was ringing in the pocket of Lieutenant Raymond Lindsay's jacket.

SIX

Lieutenant Lindsay had concluded, temporarily, his investigation of the crime scene at the airport.

He searched unsuccessfully for witnesses, then talked to the security guard who made the initial call regarding the bombing. The guard in turn led him to a small car rental agency inside the airport terminal where the driver of the red convertible worked as a sales clerk.

After questioning the young man about his role in the bombing, Lindsay asked about his knowledge of the lady in the yellow dress and the similarities he had found between his convertible and the Mercedes that tried to run down Wiley and Brensley in the parking garage.

His questions didn't produce the answers he expected. The clerk disavowed knowing anything about the bombing, the woman, the Mercedes, or its owners. When asked where he got his car, he said he didn't know, other than his father purchased it from a used car lot at a dealership. He didn't know the name of the dealer or where it was located.

Lindsay suspected the clerk knew more about where the Mercedes and his convertible came from than he was admitting. He would look into the department of motor vehicle records of both vehicles and see what the connection was.

He would also look into the backgrounds of the young man and the woman in the yellow dress to further reveal any connections there might be. Then he would question the clerk again. Having the answers before he asked the questions was always more effective when he knew the answers before he asked the questions.

His interrogation was interrupted by a phone call from the precinct dispatcher, notifying him of a shooting on the outskirts of Westland.

"Did you say Lorraine Brensley?" he exclaimed when told of Lorraine's involvement in the shooting. "Like in George Brensley?"

"His wife," the dispatcher said. "And another woman."

Lindsay considered letting the dispatcher give the call to another officer to investigate, then deciding the clerk was no more of a flight risk than Brensley and Wiley, quickly changed his mind. Hoping all three men would still be around in the morning, he concluded his investigation, told the clerk not to leave town, and left the airport without him.

"Any casualties?" he asked the dispatcher as he swung his car out of the airport, onto the freeway, and headed toward the foothills.

"No," came the reply. "Just a car shot up."

In spite of the seriousness of the situation, Lindsay laughed out loud. "What the hell are the Brensleys up to now?" he asked himself and the dispatcher. He didn't have an answer, and neither did the dispatcher.

The possibility that George Brensley and Jim Wiley were involved with organized crime had crossed his mind when he first saw the burning remains of the bombed Buick in the airport parking garage. Actually, it had more than crossed his mind, it had stayed there for quite a while, but the more he talked to them, the more his suspicions disappeared.

"Nah," he finally said to himself. The intuition he had gathered from his years in law enforcement very seldom let him down, and he was convinced the two men were telling the truth.

Now he was beginning to wonder again. From the report he had been given, it appeared that a considerable number of shots had been fired from a semiautomatic weapon and at least one pistol. That, and the bombing, were usually the type of activities carried out by organized crime or drug dealers.

The question was, why would the mob be interested in an international businessman and an attorney, along with the attorney's wife and another person in her car. Wiley, or both men, must have done something that displeased someone. Or maybe one of them had information that somebody didn't want repeated. The mob had killed for less.

But why Brensley's wife, and the other woman. Organized crime usually left women alone, or at least they did in the old days. Times had changed and not for the better. Now just about anyone could be a target.

Twenty minutes had passed when the illuminated steeple of Reverend Baldwin's church came into view. Other police officers were already on the scene and the flashing lights from their squad cars filled the night with alternating streaks of blue and red.

Curious neighbors and choir members were also milling around or leaning against their vehicles as they discussed the excitement that Lorraine and Jennifer had brought into their otherwise quiet evening.

Lindsay climbed out of his squad car and walked slowly around Jennifer's bullet riddled auto. He exchanged a few words with officers who had been taking notes, tapped a tire with the toe of a shoe as though thinking about purchasing, gave the car a sympathetic shake of his head, then approached the two women.

"Your car has some holes in it."

"A few," Lorraine answered.

"Are you Lorraine Brensley?"

"Yes."

He looked at Jennifer. "And you?"

"Jennifer Brookbaine."

He looked at each of them again, trying to decide where he had seen them. "I believe I've met you somewhere?" he said to Lorraine.

"I'm a prosecuting attorney for the City of Westland," Lorraine informed him when there was no indication from Lindsay as to where they had met.

"Oh . . ." Lindsay shrugged as though it didn't mean much to him, then turned to Jennifer. "And you?"

"Private investigator."

The lieutenant's eyes scanned the low cut red dress and high heels that Jennifer was wearing. "Humm . . . I recognize you. The last time I saw you was in a jail cell through some bars. I believe they picked you up for being a hooker or something."

Jennifer smirked. "I was in the middle of an investigation."

"Is that what they're calling it now?"

Before Jennifer could offer a retort, he moved his attention back to Lorraine. "And now I know where I saw you. I believe you were giving her advice on how to avoid the charges."

"Did she manage to get you out?" he asked Jennifer.

Jennifer's gaze left the lieutenant's face, and moved slowly down to his advancing waistline.

"And now I remember where I last saw you. A coffee shop downtown. I believe you were ordering a custard cream filled donut, or was it a chocolate filled eclair sprinkled with sugar dust."

Lindsay's expression didn't change. He had heard most of the donut jokes. "It was probably the chocolate eclair sprinkled with sugar dust. I heard that chocolate is good for you."

He returned his attention to Lorraine. "I think I've met your husband."

"George?"

"Yes."

"In court?"

"No. He was having some car trouble at the airport. He was still there the last time I saw him."

"Did you help him?"

"Not exactly."

"Did he get his car going?"

"It was going, all right."

He looked at the dents and what was left of the damaged hood of Jennifer's sports car. "Did you see who put these here?"

"Jennifer did, when she ran into the rear end of the Mercedes?"

Lindsay's eyebrows raised. "Mercedes?"

"Yes. She pushed it off the road at the hairpin curve back there."

"With this??!!"

"Yes."

"Did it do any damage to the Mercedes?"

"About as much as my bullets."

"So you returned fire."

"Yes."

"Any damage?"

"No. I got the feeling my bullets were bouncing off the windshield."

"So you carry a gun."

"Yes."

"What kind?"

Lorraine lifted her twenty-two caliber five-shot pistol out of her handbag.

Lindsay gave a condescending crooked grin and cupped his hands a few inches apart in front of him as if to say, "Is that all you had?"

"It fits inside my purse, and it does

everything I ask it to. Do you have something against it?"

"No, no, not at all. I used to carry one of those as a spare. It fit inside my watch pocket. Have you ever had to use it?"

"Before tonight?"

"Sure. Why not before tonight. Have you ever had to use your twenty-two caliber, five-shot pistol, before tonight? Before you gunned down the Mercedes."

Lorraine was becoming defensive. "Just once. A gentleman that I had prosecuted confronted me in a parking lot one day and asked me the same question you're asking. He wanted to know if I thought a bullet from, this, little ol' thing, would stop him. I told him maybe not, but I figured five of them might slow him down a little. He must have agreed because he decided to wait for the police to arrive."

Lindsay didn't have an answer. He gave a semi-positive shrug of his head, then looked at Jennifer. "Do you carry a gun?"

"Of course."

"What kind?"

"A thirty-eight."

A more positive, "Ah . . ." was forthcoming. "And you need yours for . . . ?"

Jennifer didn't speak. Instead, she cocked

her head, opened her arms, and gestured toward the bullet holes in her car.

"Did your bullets do any damage?" Lindsay asked.

"I wasn't firing. She was."

He returned to Lorraine. "Did the bullets from her thirty-eight do any damage?"

Lorraine's voice had a tinge of satisfaction as she spoke. "No. Jennifer's bullets were also bouncing off the windshield, and the back window, and the side window, and everything else on the Mercedes that I shot at."

"Did you see the shooters?"

"Just one, but we're reasonably sure there were at least two of them. A woman, and maybe a man."

The lieutenant's eyebrows raised again. "By any chance was the woman wearing a yellow dress?"

"As a matter of fact, she was. How did you know that?"

He didn't answer the question. "Did you get a look at their faces?"

"No. The last time we saw them, the car was surrounded by dust and we were in a hurry to get out of there."

"Did you get a license plate number."

Lorraine handed him a slip of paper with the plate number.

Lindsay studied the number, then opened his note pad to where he had written information connecting the Mercedes to the red convertible that had set off the bomb in George's car at the airport.

"Interesting," he murmured to himself.

"Is the number important?" Lorraine asked.

He ignored her request. "Can you describe the car?"

"It was a Mercedes . . ."

"Like a limo?"

"Yes, like a limo."

"Grey in color?"

"How did you know that?"

"Most Mercedes are grey. Are you two involved with organized crime in any way?"

"Why do you ask?"

"Oh, I don't know. I talked to a couple other guys a little while ago who I thought might be in organized crime." His voice became a little sterner. "For a short time I wondered if I would have to take them in for questioning and lock them up."

Lorraine got the message. "Well, we're not in organized crime, and you're not taking us anywhere and locking us up." Her voice also became a little sterner. She enunciated each word. "Like I told you, I'm a . . . Prosecuting Attorney . . . for the City of Westland."

The lieutenant didn't seem any more impressed than the first time he heard it.

"And a darned good one," Jennifer added.

Lindsay's gaze moved again to the red dress that Jennifer enjoyed wearing, then back to Lorraine. "And is it part of a prosecuting attorney's job to help hookers, excuse me, ladies of the evening, excuse me, investigators to get out of jail."

"Jennifer is not a hooker," Lorraine replied. "She just likes to dress that way."

Jennifer came to her aid. "Lorraine does more than just get hookers out of jail. She almost convicted a piece of scum today."

"Almost . . . ?"

"She would have too, if your police department had held onto a couple of witnesses."

"The Lennie Barnes case?"

"That's it."

"Yeah, I know about it. They found your witnesses out in the desert."

"Were they dead?"

"Pretty much."

The lieutenant didn't offer more particulars. Before they could inquire further, he continued, "The people in the car that was chasing you, do you have any idea who they might have been?"

"We wondered if the woman in the yellow dress might be Lennie Barnes' sister," Lorraine replied. "We saw her in court today, and she was wearing a yellow dress. And the other person in the car might have been Lennie Barnes himself. But like we said, we couldn't get a good look at them through the dust."

Lindsay nodded in partial agreement. "I'll have a look where they went off the road. Maybe they left something behind . . . like the front end of your automobile."

For the next several minutes he asked questions about the altercation with the Mercedes. His interrogation slowly changed from how it happened to why it happened.

He eyed them a little more intently, thinking of George Brensley and Jim Wiley, and George's bombed Buick. "Are you sure you don't know anybody in organized crime? Lawyers and private investigators sometimes do little favors for the mob, and then when the mob has no more use for them, they find themselves dispensable."

"I'm sure we all know somebody in organized crime," Lorraine answered. "We just haven't discovered yet that they're in organized crime. The only one we're acquainted with at present is Lennie Barnes. He's a low life street thug who's in the illegal drug business and getting unfortunate kids addicted, but I wouldn't be surprised if he's involved with someone higher. He seemed to have a lot of help at his trial."

"I don't mean to put you in the syndicate," Lindsay said. "And I'm certain, reasonably certain, you're not." His glance moved again to Jennifer's red dress and then back to Lorraine. "I mean, it's just that this sort of thing is normally not done by your local dime store hoodlums. They prefer a Saturday night special in a dark alley. The mob, on the other hand, enjoys a good gun fight. Or blowing someone up in a parking lot."

"Of course they also enjoy shooting a leader of a rival gang after a good meal in a fine restaurant. I don't suppose you two might have enjoyed a good meal in a fine restaurant this evening. Which one of you do you think they might have been after?"

Jennifer shrugged.

Lorraine nodded. "Probably me."

"Do you happen to know a guy by the name of Jim Wiley?"

"He's a friend. Why are you interested in Jim?"

"No reason. And your husband is George Brensley?"

"Why are you asking about George?"

"No reason."

Lindsay went back to searching the car with his flashlight.

"Anything in particular you're looking for?" Jennifer asked.

"A bullet. Something I can give my police chief to prove I've been working. Just be happy I'm not collecting it from the Medical Examiner."

He shone his flashlight around the interior and then under the seats. There were no bullets. Instead he pulled out a dusty and weathered piece of paper that had obviously been there a long time. It crackled as he unfolded it. Inside he discovered a sales agreement.

"Rental vehicle?" he asked.

"No," Jennifer replied. "It's a one owner low mileage car I purchased today from an auto dealership downtown."

"Would you like me to tell you who the one owner of your car really is?"

"Who?"

"According to this form, a car rental company that I visited tonight at the airport."

"No."

"Yes."

"No."

"Yes.

"No. The salesman at the car lot where I purchased it said it was a one owner Cream Puff that belonged to a long time steady customer."

"Was she also a little old lady who only drove it on Sundays?"

"I don't know."

"I hate to disappoint you, but the loyal long time one owner steady customer who owned your Cream Puff was actually the car rental company itself."

"No??!!"

"Yes. I've heard that sometimes, when rental cars become too high mileage, or have had the, excuse me, crap driven out of them, rental companies ship them off to a used car lot. Some of these lots like to turn back the mileage and sell them to unsuspecting idio . . . excuse me again, customers as a low mileage one owner, instead of what they really are, a high mileage, one thousand driver."

"How do you know this?"

"I bought one once from a used car dealer. Probably everybody has bought one at one time or another. It drove beautifully, for two days, then it began to blow smoke, burn oil, lose power . . ."

Lorraine was nodding in agreement. "That would explain the blue smoke, lack of power going up the hill, coughing and wheezing just before Jennifer's car died, and the . . ."

"Are you going to look for the people who tried to kill us?" Jennifer asked.

"I'll be looking," Lindsay replied, "although their Mercedes is probably getting new licence plates and a paint job by now, and your shooters will be in a barroom or pool hall somewhere with five or six witnesses claiming they've been right there with them all night."

The lieutenant circled the remains of the Cream Puff one more time. After inspecting the interior and exterior, he paused at the rear of the car and shone his flashlight on a bullet riddled temporary cardboard identification card that was attached to it.

"Do you have the name of the dealer where you bought your vehicle?" he asked.

"Sandstorm Automotive and Used Car Sales," Jennifer replied. "Why?"

"No reason," Lindsay answered. "You just reminded me, I need to have another talk with a car rental clerk at the airport."

SEVEN

The evening was getting late. Although Lieutenant Lindsay had informed Jim Wiley and George Brensley they could leave, curiosity and a desire to learn anything that could help them understand why George's Buick had been bombed kept them at the airport.

Lindsay was no longer in the parking garage. After talking to the security officer who arrived shortly after the explosion, he and the officer entered an elevator that went down to the departures and arrivals levels.

Jim and George continued to watch as the bomb squad and forensics team sifted through one piece of evidence and then another until they had finished their investigation. Finally, the yellow police tapes were removed from around the burned out cars and a salvage team began loading what was left of them onto trailers for their trip to the police compound and further investigation.

As Lindsay had done earlier, they examined both vehicles, paying additional attention to the young man's convertible, searching for the evidence the lieutenant appeared to have discovered that he neglected to share with them.

"I think I might have found it," George exclaimed as he passed the rear of a trailer where the convertible was being loaded.

Ignoring an operator's warnings to stay clear, he wiped blackened soot away and examined more closely the barely visible burned over numbers on the license plate.

"I see it," Jim said. "The first three numbers on the convertible's license plate are the same as the first three numbers on the Mercedes that tried to run us down, and the last three letters are almost identical. They look like they could have come from the same place. Now we know what Lindsay was interested in."

"A connection between the driver of the convertible and the lady in the yellow dress," George replied. "And we know where he went to get the answer."

Like Lindsay and the security officer before them, they took an elevator to the arrivals level where they had been told the owner of the convertible was employed and where they suspected Lindsay had gone.

The lieutenant was nowhere to be seen. They caught sight of the security officer briefly as he passed through the baggage claim area, then he disappeared inside an elevator that went back up to the parking garage.

Backtracking along the path where they had first spotted the officer took them through the baggage area and to a row of car rental agencies that lined a wall nearby. They passed the larger companies which had long lines of vacationers and business people waiting for vehicles, and to a smaller less busy desk at the end of the row.

"See someone familiar?" George asked. "So this is where he works. A clerk at a car rental company. But I don't see the lieutenant."

In the parking lot the young man had worn jeans and a T-shirt, but now he was dressed in a uniform which included a navy blue blazer, gray slacks, and a white shirt and red tie. He smiled an inquisitive smile when he saw them.

"Welcome to Sandstorm Auto Rentals," he said as he moved the souvenir he had picked up from George's Buick to a more prominent position on the counter. "Did you lose your car? Do you perhaps need a new one?"

"Yeah, we need a new one," George answered. "But first, we need to ask you some questions. Was a Lieutenant Lindsay here to see you?"

"Briefly," the young man replied.

"Did you enjoy your conversation?"

"As far as it went. He was only here about five minutes, and he didn't ask me much. He wanted to know something about the license plate on my car."

"And?"

"And then he left."

"Why?"

"He got a telephone call, something about a gunfight north of the city. He stopped with the questioning, ordered me not to leave town in case he wanted to talk to me again, then took off in a hurry out of the terminal."

The young man opened his arms and gestured to his surroundings and the job he performed as a desk clerk. "Like I could afford to leave town."

His expression changed to amusement. "Why are you here? Oh yes, you still think I drove all the way to work today just so I could run into your car, set off your dynamite, and destroy my new paint job."

"Yeah, I'm still thinking about it," George said. "We need to ask you the same questions the lieutenant was probably asking, like why the license plate number on your convertible and the license plate number on the Mercedes that was involved in the bombing are almost identical, and what the connection is between you and the lady who planted the dynamite."

The clerk shrugged his shoulders. "There is no connection, and as far as I know, I've never met the lady, or anyone else who planted a bomb."

"Where did you buy your car?"

"I didn't buy it. Like I said when I saw you in the parking garage, and what I told the lieutenant, my father gave it to me."

"Where did your father buy it?"

"I don't know that either. I think it might have been from a car dealer somewhere."

"Is there anything you do know?"

"I know not to drive around with dynamite in my car."

George shared a look of disgusted amusement with Jim, then returned to the clerk. "There must be a reason why the license plate on the Mercedes is almost identical to the plate on your car."

"I didn't know they were identical. Maybe they both came from the same car lot."

"Or here?" George suggested.

"Maybe here, or maybe one of the other rental companies."

Jim spread out a piece of paper where he had recorded the licence numbers. "Was your convertible one of these?"

The clerk entered the licence plate numbers into his computer. "What do you know," he said. "My car was originally from here, but it was terminated."

"Interesting description. Why terminated?"

"I don't know. They do the same thing with employees. No longer in service. They do that to anything that becomes too old or too high mileage to use or rent."

"Do you know the name of the used car lot where your car went?"

"My computer doesn't say. Probably the company's dealership downtown, but they could go to any one of several dealers around the state."

"What about the Mercedes' licence plate number?"

"There's no record of it in my computer."

"Do you carry Mercedes Benz limos here?"

"Of course."

"Who rents them?"

"Mostly people who come in from their corporate offices in other states, sometimes other countries, and they want a luxury vehicle."

"Why doesn't your computer show a record of it being rented?"

"Regular Mercedes show up. But a few are in our exclusive high dollar and fleet division. They're for people who are looking for added features, or expect discretion such as their being in town kept confidential. This could be one of those."

"What kind of confidential?"

"A couple ladies in the back seat, meetings that aren't supposed to be taking place, added protection."

"Protection?"

"Sometimes they want one that offers protection. Armor plating and such."

"Armor plating . . . ? In Westland . . . ?"

"The people who rent them don't always stay in Westland. They go to other cities, sometimes other states, and Mexico."

"Why Mexico?"

"Search me. I don't know. Probably on business."

"It's not unusual," Jim explained. "We have manufacturing facilities there, just over the border. So do a lot of other electronics and automotive companies, and visiting executives often hire limousines to take them around."

George stared at the clerk for an answer, and then at Jim. "But why armor plating?"

The clerk shrugged.

Jim shook his head. "I've never heard of anyone wanting a vehicle with armor plating, at least not in Westland. The areas where we have plants, here or across the border, don't need an armored Mercedes, or any other armored vehicle. The occupants of these vehicles must be going into some very unsavory locations and meeting some very unsavory people."

"Organized crime?"

"Maybe. Maybe Lieutenant Lindsay was right. Maybe we're involved with organized crime, and don't know it."

"Have you ever seen the people who rent one of these Mercedes limos," George asked the clerk.

"Sure. I've seen them pick it up at our rental lot at the edge of the airport. A man and a woman."

"Is the woman blond and wears a yellow dress?"

"Ah," the clerk said. "Now I see the connection you were looking for. She's blond. Her clothing varies. The man is a gaudily dressed, arrogant, flashy type cowboy, and he doesn't treat her with very much respect. For that matter, he doesn't treat our employees or anybody else with very much respect either."

"Is the Mercedes for them?" Jim asked.

"No. I've been told they pick it up for other people who arrive in a private jet, off a runway that's away from the terminal."

"Do you know where the jet originates?"

"No. You could ask someone higher up in

our company who keeps records of such things, but I doubt if they'll tell you."

"We'll ask anyway," George said. "How many of these vehicles do you rent?"

"More than you would think. I can ask Fleet to get one for you, if you like."

"No thanks. A Buick, or something like it, will do, if you have one."

Being reminded what his job was, the clerk entered more information into his computer, dialed a number, and waited for a lot attendant to respond.

The mischievous smile returned to his face. "If you like, I'll tell them to find one that doesn't have a bomb in it."

"Scariest damned thing I ever got involved with," George exclaimed as they drove away from the airport.

"The bomb in your car?"

"That car rental clerk. I'm not sure I'll ever want to rent another vehicle after talking to him. Any idea why those people in the Mercedes would want to get rid of us?"

"Not a clue. I suppose it could be one angry lady taking Wiley Electronics for everything she can, or an international crime syndicate using the company for their own illegal purposes, or anything in between. What I am sure of is that one of us got close to something that got someone's attention, and it made us targets to get rid of."

"And now," George said, "all we have to do is discover what it is."

EIGHT

The Brensley's home was located on a narrow road that curved back and forth along the foothills of a mountain range above the desert. It was a compromise that George and Lorraine had made years earlier when they were first married and moved from the sprawling peacefulness of the southwestern cattle country where they were raised, to the City of Westland to practice law.

Their closest neighbors were ranchers who raised their cattle on the grass of the higher elevations, a variety of coyotes, roadrunners and other desert creatures that wandered in and out of their properties, a few city slickers who enjoyed the peacefulness the area offered, and Reverend Baldwin's church which was a quarter mile away. From the church parking lot the lights of downtown Westland were easily visible in the distance.

Lieutenant Lindsay had left the church to examine the area where the Mercedes went off the road. He was gazing along the narrow beam of light from his flashlight when Jim Wiley and George Brensley approached in their rental vehicle.

Wondering what had brought him to their neighborhood when he was supposed to be investigating a gunfight, George braked to a stop. Jim rolled down a window.

"Lieutenant."

"Wiley."

"Lieutenant."

"Brensley."

"Troubles?" Jim asked.

"You might say that."

"At the church?"

"There, and here," the lieutenant replied. "Brensley's wife was in a bit of an altercation with another car. Another woman was with her. Don't worry, they're both okay. They might still be at the church. I'll let them tell you about it."

Past experience and Lindsay's reluctance to share information told them there would probably be no more explanations forthcoming. They left him to ponder whatever it was that he was pondering, and sped toward the church.

As they neared, Reverend Baldwin, his armed congregation, and curious onlookers in the parking lot came into view. In the middle of it all stood Lorraine and Jennifer.

Lorraine was watching the glimmering lights of the city through the on and off glow of lights from police cars when she noticed a vehicle approaching the entrance to the church parking lot. She continued to observe as it turned into the driveway and came to a stop near choir members who were standing beside their pickup trucks, their rifles and pistols still at the ready.

Her husband and Jim Wiley climbed out of the car and walked the short distance to where she and Jennifer were talking to Reverend Baldwin.

"Reverend." George's salutation was partly a greeting and partly a question.

"George," Baldwin responded warmly.

"Lorraine?" This time George's salutation was a complete question.

"Hi honey." Lorraine gave him a hug that was longer and tighter than usual.

"Jennifer? I didn't expect to see you tonight."

"Hi George. You were going to the airport after work, and I wanted Lorraine to see my new car, so I gave her a ride home. Besides, she was feeling a little blue after her trial today and could use some company."

"I heard about the verdict," George sympathized. "I'm sorry."

"I'm getting over it," Lorraine answered. She released her husband and put her arms around Jim Wiley. "Hi Jim. It's so good to see you."

Jim hugged back. "It's good to see you too. I'm sorry about your trial."

"I'll have another trial. Oh, excuse me. Jim, this our friend, Jennifer Brookbaine. Jennifer, this is George's and my friend, Jim Wiley."

Jennifer had been watching. She examined Jim a little more closely, then looked at Lorraine.

"My new husband . . . ? How come you haven't introduced him to me before?"

Jim had also been watching. He gazed a little longer than necessary at the curves in Jennifer's red dress. "A pleasure to meet you. George said that Lorraine had us dating. I don't remember the wedding, but I'm sure I would have remembered you. How long have we known each other? Are we happy? Are you keeping your name? Do we have children?"

"Not yet." Jennifer pointed a thumb in George and Lorraine's direction. "Unless you count those two."

Jim turned to his friends. "Why haven't you introduced us before?"

George smirked. "We didn't want to start a fire. Where's this new car that Jennifer couldn't wait for Lorraine to see?"

"Right over there," Lorraine said, opening her arms and gesturing to what was left of the Cream Puff.

The only noticeable glass in the car was the windshield which was splattered with bullet holes. Most of what remained of the side and rear windows had fallen out somewhere between the altercation on the highway and Reverend Baldwin's church. Holes and dents dotted the metal, and the front end was bashed in where it had collided with the rear of the Mercedes when Jennifer forced it off the road. Steam and oil had, for the most part, ceased to spit from the engine, mostly because there was nothing left to spit.

George's mouth gaped open as he stared at the holes. "I hope this belongs to some other people."

"No. It's Jennifer's. She just got it today. Isn't it a beauty."

"Very nice . . . I suppose. If I ever decide to buy what appears to be a bullet riddled sports car with no windows and no front end, lying in a pool of black oil, this would be one of my first choices."

George looked toward the choir members who still had their weapons at the ready. "Who did this? Don't tell me Reverend Baldwin's congregation . . ."

"Of course not," Lorraine said. "It happened on the way home."

George stared at Jennifer for an answer. When none was forthcoming, he looked at his wife again, then at the armed choir members, and finally at Reverend Baldwin. "Is the church having some problems?"

"Reverend Baldwin and his congregation saved our lives tonight," Lorraine explained.

"Think nothing of it," Baldwin replied. "It was the neighborly thing to do. Are you sure you'll be alright?"

"We'll be fine now," Lorraine replied. "Thank you again."

"The neighborly thing to do?"

George watched in puzzlement as rifles were returned to their racks in pickup trucks and their drivers slowly began to disperse from the parking lot around them. "Since when do you need Reverend Baldwin and his choir to save your lives? And what is Lieutenant Lindsay doing at the curve down the road?" he asked.

"You know Lieutenant Lindsay?"

"We've met. I'll tell you what he means to us as soon as you tell us what he means to you. He said you were in some kind of altercation with another car."

"As you see, we had a little trouble on the way home," Lorraine said. "And the reverend and his choir offered to help us out. Somebody took some shots at us. Lieutenant Lindsay came to investigate."

George stared again at the bullet riddled vehicle, and ran his hand over some holes. "Are these what you refer to as . . . some shots?"

"I'm afraid so."

"And you were in it?"

"Jennifer was driving. I was shooting at the Mercedes. We think it was bullet proof. I got their licence plate number."

"Did you say Mercedes?" George exclaimed.

Jim looked at the information Lorraine had written. "It could be the same car we saw at the airport. The licence plate has been changed, but it's similar to the Mercedes that tried to run us down, and the convertible that ran into your Buick and set off the bomb in your engine compartment."

George was quiet.

Lorraine wasn't.

" . . . bomb . . . ?"

George was quiet a moment longer. "Remember when I said we were having a slight problem with the Buick."

"Yes . . . ?"

"It was a little more than a slight problem. Somebody put a bomb in my car."

"A bomb!!??"

"A bomb. But Jim discovered it before it went off."

"That's good to know."

"At first."

"What do you mean, at first . . . ?"

"It eventually went off, but we weren't in it at the time."

"I can see that. Where were you?"

"I think we might have been hiding behind a pickup truck of some kind. That was where we were when Jim grabbed the guy who set off the bomb."

"So you caught the person who planted the bomb."

"No. I suspected he was involved. Jim thinks he just set it off by accident. The people who really put the bomb in the engine compartment got away. They were driving a Mercedes, maybe the same one that was after you."

Lorraine stood quietly in puzzled shock for a moment, then, "I think you'd better start at the beginning. And don't leave anything out this time."

This time George didn't leave anything out, telling Lorraine and Jennifer everything that had happened to them since he met Jim at the airport.

"Did you say a blond woman in a yellow dress?" Lorraine asked when he described the woman Jim had seen running away from his car.

"Yes."

"Is this the same woman in a yellow dress who works in Wiley Electronics accounting department, who is Lennie Barnes' sister and was in court with him today, who we think was in the Mercedes that ambushed us on the highway and filled Jennifer's car full of bullet holes, and who Jennifer and I believe could be involved, along with her brother, with the disappearance of the money from Jim's company? Is this the Linda Barnes you're referring to?"

"It's beginning to look that way."

"I can understand why Lennie wouldn't like me," Lorraine said, "but what could he possibly have against you and George? Unless, maybe he thought I was the one who was picking you up at the airport."

"Except it was your husband's car that was bombed," Jim said. "Would he try to get to you through George?"

"Maybe. He's sick enough to do something like that, although I suppose it could have been any of us, or all of us that he was after. But why? Why wouldn't he come after me directly? On second thought, I guess he did come after me directly. And Jennifer."

"Well, I'm going to find out," Jim said. "I'm going down to the plant tonight when no one is in the office and have a look in the area where Linda Barnes works. If she is involved, maybe she left something lying around."

George shook his head. "Except you won't be going there by yourself. I'll be coming with you."

"No," Jim exclaimed. "I'm not going to put you into any more danger. Wiley Electronics is my business, and I'm going to get to the bottom of it."

"Oh no," George replied. "This is also my business. Those bastards made it my business when they planted their bomb in my car and tried to kill my wife."

"And Jennifer," Lorraine reminded them. "We will also be coming. We have a score to settle with Mister Lennie Barnes and his sister, and somewhere in her department, we're going to find the answer."

"I think I might have found one answer you've been looking for," Jennifer said as she took a long last sentimental look at her recently deceased Cream Puff. "A connection between all the vehicles we've seen tonight. The temporary licence identification card on my car is almost identical to licence plates on the other three cars. The connection could be the dealer where I made my purchase."

"Sandstorm Automotive and Used Car Sales."

NINE

Wiley Electronics was a sprawling ten acre complex on the northeast edge of Westland. It consisted of a four-story office building where management, sales and accounting, engineering and design were located, and other structures that contained assembly lines, manufacturing, inventory, maintenance and shipping. To enter, visitors and employees had to pass a security station at the main entrance.

The evening was quiet and late enough that most employees had gone home. The only automobiles in the parking lot belonged to shipping personnel who were finishing loading trucks, a small van with a security company's insignia on the side . . .

. . . and one very large grey Mercedes Benz limo with a license plate they recognized.

George stopped his rented sedan sideways and close to the Mercedes, blocking its only escape route. While he and Lorraine inspected the vehicle, Jim and Jennifer walked the short distance to the security building and approached the guard on duty.

"Could you tell us who's driving the Mercedes?" Jim asked.

The night watchman finished ogling the centerfold in a magazine he was pretending to read. Without bothering to close it, he eyed them with a certain amount of disdain.

"Who wants to know?"

Giving herself a job she had not yet been formally offered, Jennifer answered. "I'm an investigator employed by the company. And this is Jim Wiley."

When the guard didn't react, she continued. "He owns this place."

The guard was about twenty-five years old and appeared to be new to his profession. He was dressed in the brown uniform of an outside security company, and up to that point didn't seem to be overly concerned about his job. He looked at Jim for a few seconds, then nervously began straightening his tie. He closed the magazine and slipped it into a drawer.

"Oh, hello Mr. Wiley. I didn't recognize you at first. Linda Barnes drives the Mercedes. She works in the purchasing department."

"Does she always work late?" Jennifer asked.

"Sometimes. Almost everyone works late at one time or another. She seems to put in more hours than most, although this seems to be a little later than usual. Is there some reason you're asking?"

"Just curious. Maybe that's how she can afford a Mercedes."

"I think it belongs to someone else. She just drives it to work every once in a while, that's all."

"Were you here when she came in?" Jim asked.

"Yeah. She came in about half an hour ago."

"Was anybody with her?"

"Like who?"

"Oh, I don't know. Maybe a boyfriend, or a brother?"

The security guard shrugged. "Don't recall seeing anybody like that."

"Is this the only way in?"

"As far as I know. This is where my security company put me, and this is the only entrance I'm familiar with, or care about."

"I'm surprised you don't care more about who comes in with employees," Jennifer exclaimed. "Are you sure no one was with her? A cowboy type person?"

The guard shook his head. "Don't recall ever seeing a cowboy type person."

"Isn't it your job to notice those things?"

"When I took this job, I wasn't informed that checking on guests who arrive with employees was in my job description."

Jennifer nodded. "Ah, I see. Maybe if I call your company, someone there could tell me what your job description is. Maybe your boss. Or maybe the Westland Police Department could help us. I'm sure they have a record of your job description from the background check they obtained for your security clearance and license to be a security guard."

When this information was met with an indifference shrug and no apparent fear of authority, Jennifer pointed toward Lorraine.

"Or, do you see that woman over there. She's a prosecuting attorney for the City of Westland, and I'll bet she could tell you what your job description is. Maybe here or maybe down at police headquarters. If you like, I could ask her to accompany you down there for some questions."

The guard appeared to think it over, then glanced at Lorraine and George who were on their hands and knees, searching for desert grass under the Mercedes. Still not impressed, he dismissed this threat with another indifferent shrug.

"Whoever questions you, it shouldn't take more than six or seven hours."

Time didn't appear to be of importance.

Jennifer decided it was time to adjust the truth a little. "I heard that a couple witnesses for the Lennie Barnes trial today were taken down to the precinct for questioning, and then they disappeared.   Rumor has it their acquaintances took them out to the desert and filled them full of bullets."

The guard's head stopped shrugging. He had apparently heard of the Lennie Barnes trial and the two witnesses who were missing.

Finally a weakness. "If you like," Jennifer said, "I'll call my friend over, and she and some police officers can take you downtown and get this all straightened out. Are you sure Linda Barnes was alone when she came in?"

Some of the guard's memory began to return. "Oh. Maybe there was a man with her. But I never saw him before."

"What did he look like?"

"I don't know. I didn't pay that much attention to him. Average build, average height, five foot ten or eleven."

"That's the best you can do? Average? Like almost everybody in the city?"

"Maybe he was a cowboy type person."

"I just gave you that description. Are you sure he was dressed like a cowboy?"

The guard shrugged. "Could be. Like I said, I didn't get a really good look at him."

"LORRAINE!!!!"

More of the guard's memory returned.

"Yeah, yeah, a cowboy type person. I'm pretty sure he might have been a cowboy type person."

"You're sure he might have been, or you're sure he was, a cowboy type person?"

"I'm sure he was."

"Give me a name."

The guard's shoulders stopped. He held them in a frozen shrug. "I can't."

"Why not?"

"I'm just trying to stay out of jail, or the desert with those two other guys you told me about. And I was only paying attention to Linda."

"Are you afraid of the man who was with her?"

There was a nervous, "Of course not," from the guard. His ashen appearance indicated otherwise.

"Would you recognize him if you saw him again?"

"Maybe."

"What about his clothes? Did you notice what he was wearing?"

"Like what?"

"Like outlandish attire, like a gaudy cowboy type shirt, multi colored cowboy boots, a cowboy hat . . . ?"

"Yeah, yeah. Outlandish attire, like a gaudy cowboy type shirt, multi colored cowboy boots, and a cowboy hat. Yes. Definitely a cowboy hat."

"You're still just repeating everything I say to you. What was Linda wearing?"

"A yellow dress. Quite a looker."

"At least you got something right. Are you sure about her brother and what he was wearing?"

The guard didn't respond to the bait. Instead, he opened his hands, palms up, over his desk, in a gesture of helpless, incompetent ignorance. "I don't know if he was her brother."

After that he was silent.

While Jennifer continued, unsuccessfully, to get the guard to admit the identity of the man who went in with Linda Barnes, Jim was dialing the number at police headquarters that Lieutenant Lindsay had given them at the airport. Lindsay wasn't in. The dispatcher said he was on another investigation but that he would try to contact him. He came back on the line a few seconds later.

"Lieutenant Lindsay will be coming," he said. "I told him I could send out another officer, but when I gave him your name and told him who was with you, he insisted on taking the call."

"Maybe he's beginning to like us."

A slight laughter came through the phone. "Or his curiosity is getting the best of him. He said he wants to see who else might be trying to kill you tonight. He also said to tell your two lady friends not to shoot anyone and he would be there in fifteen minutes."

Fifteen minutes later, Lieutenant Lindsay arrived.

Lorraine and George had finished inspecting the Mercedes for damages that would identify it as the vehicle Jennifer had run off the road. Other than a few scratches on the rear bumper where she had destroyed the front end of her newly purchased, used, one owner, rental company's Cream Puff, and some slight scars on the windshield where bullets had bounced off, there was not much to see.

"I suppose they'll have to run out of numbers sooner or later," he quipped, looking at the hastily fastened screws that held the newly installed, similarly numbered licence plate.

George nodded a greeting. "We thought you would be home in bed by now."

"Not likely. I was on my way back to the airport when this call came in, and I couldn't help myself. I had to see if you were still alive."

Lorraine looked past him as if expecting other police cars to arrive. "Didn't you bring any help with you?"

Lindsay shook his head. "Nope. Just me. We don't know yet what's waiting for us. It could be something, it could be nothing. And with the shortage of police officers we've been having lately, and everybody out on other assignments, my chief usually doesn't move unless there's been a killing."

"What does she call George and Jim getting their car blown up and Jennifer and me getting shot at?"

"A spat between a couple of crime families. Don't worry about the chief. She thinks that everybody's in organized crime. It's the times we live in. Are your shooters and bombers inside?"

"We think so," Jim replied. "The security guard wasn't saying much, but he confirmed that the driver of the Mercedes is Linda Barnes. She works in the accounting department. The guard wasn't too free with other information, but we believe there is a man with her who is probably her brother."

"Well, let's find out. What floor does this Linda Barnes work on?"

"The fourth," Jim said, "and I'll be coming with you. I know where the purchasing offices are."

"And I've been to where her desk is located," George said. "I'll be coming too."

Lindsay raised a finger in protest, then deciding he could use the assistance, motioned for them to follow.

Lorraine and Jennifer didn't wait for an invitation. They fell in behind as the lieutenant walked toward the office building. He started to object, then deciding admonishment would do no good, gave them a weak calvary-like wave of a hand and motioned them onward.

Much of the building was in darkness except for the main reception area which was still partially illuminated. A telephone light was blinking on and off at the reception desk. It stopped before Jim could reach it. He looked toward the security building in time to see the guard hang up his phone and return to his magazine.

"Do you keep a record of calls?" Lindsay asked.

Jim nodded. "I can get it for you."

"Good. In the meantime, let's see what's happening on the fourth floor."

Ignoring the elevator, Lindsay led them to the emergency stairs and began to climb. As he prepared to open the door at the fourth floor, he held his thirty-eight in the air close beside him. His two women companions already had their guns drawn and were holding them in a similar fashion.

This time he held up a hand in a silent demand for them to stay where they were.

They obeyed, and alone he quietly made his way past the individual work stations until he neared the only one that had a desk light burning.

Lindsay had often wondered which came first, the violence or the cold feeling that swept over him and told him that something violent was about to happen.

Maybe it was the raspy moans of the wounded woman slumped over her desk, with a red splash of blood on the back of her yellow dress. Or maybe it was the knowledge that Lennie Barnes, or whoever else might have shot her could still be in the building. Or perhaps it was the intuition he had gathered over the years that let him know his own life could be in danger.

Or maybe it was all three. He just knew it was time to dive for cover.

TEN

The first bullet passed through the air where Lindsay's body had been a moment earlier. It imbedded in a wall. The second tore a hole in a partition just above his head as he ran across the narrow aisle and took cover behind a file cabinet.

He peered into the darkness, searching for the source of the gunfire. His demand to, "Stop! Police!" was met with another burst of bullets that thudded into the cabinet. Then a shadowy figure raced to the other end of the office and disappeared through an emergency doorway.

As Lindsay ran in pursuit, he yelled for his four accomplices to stay where they were and to call for an ambulance and police back up. He hesitated a moment at the door the gunmen had used to make his escape, then flung it open and rushed down the steps toward the sounds of echoing footsteps.

None of his accomplices stayed. While Lorraine ran to give aid to the wounded woman in the cubicle, George called for Emergency Medical Assistance and the Westland Police Department.

At the same time, Jim and Jennifer raced

down the stairway they had climbed on their way to the fourth floor. When they arrived at the front entrance, the intruder was already out of the building and running past the guard station toward the parking lot.

Lindsay was in pursuit. By the time he reached the parking area, the gunman was in the Mercedes and revving the engine. Then the air was filled with smoke and screeches of burning rubber as the heavy ironclad four-wheel-drive vehicle smashed into the side of George's rented sedan and spun it out of the way.

Lindsay ran to his squad car to give chase. Before he could insert the key in the ignition, the Mercedes stopped. Instead of taking the opportunity to escape, the driver turned, stepped on the accelerator, smashed into the side of George's vehicle once more and pushed it sideways along the parking lot toward him.

He fired at the tinted windshield and the invisible driver behind it until the rental sedan hit the front of his squad car and began twisting around it. Then both vehicles were being scraped backward along the asphalt.

The screeching procession temporarily came to a halt when the rear of his squad car hit a metal barrier near the security building. For a moment there was no movement, then both vehicles began rising. When the wreckage finally settled, the rear of the squad car was perched on the hood of the security van on the other side of the barrier, while the front end was firmly embedded in the side of George's rental.

The driver of the Mercedes stopped, waited a moment as if admiring his workmanship, then reversed. Not appearing to be in a hurry, he turned and drove away from the wreckage, out of the parking lot, onto the street beside the complex, and disappeared into the night.

As paramedics and police cars announced their arrival with flashing lights and wailing sirens, the lieutenant climbed down from what was left of his squad car. He directed the paramedics to the fourth floor of the office building, gave police officers a description of the escaping Mercedes, then returned to the parking lot where Jim and Jennifer were waiting near the security building.

Jennifer had emptied her pistol and was reloading.

"Hit anything?" Lindsay asked.

"I hit the Mercedes."

"Do any damage?" He already knew the answer.

"No. My bullets were bouncing off the windows."

He turned to Jim. "What about you?"

Jim was tucking the unfired five-shot-twenty-two-caliber-watch-sized pistol that Lorraine had given him before he ran down the stairs, into a pocket. "No. I already knew what would happen."

The lieutenant didn't follow up. Instead, he marched toward the security guard who was once again pretending to read the centerfold model in his magazine.

"Didn't you see what was going on around here," he demanded, partly in the authoritative voice of a disciplined police officer, and partly in the semi-scream of someone who had just had his squad car, with him and it, turned into scrap metal on top of two other vehicles.

The guard apparently hadn't shared the excitement of the experience. "Not a good look."

"Did you consider trying to stop him?"

The guard took one long last leering look at the centerfold, then slipped it into the drawer of his desk.

"Who?"

Lindsay's eyes narrowed. "Who do you think. The man that came running past your guard station."

"Are you kidding. He had a gun. Besides, my job is to keep people out, not keep them in."

"Did he look like the man that went in earlier with Linda Barnes?"

"I don't know. He went by so fast I couldn't recognize him."

"You could see his gun, but you couldn't see his face?"

"What would you see if someone was waving a gun at you?"

In response to Lindsay's glare, the guard added, "Yeah, maybe I did see somebody."

"Who?"

"A cowboy type person."

Jennifer approached. "He's just repeating information I already pried out of him. Let me give it a try."

Lindsay waved her off, like a quarterback who wasn't about to give up a play he had planned. "Do you know who you're talking to?" he said to the guard.

The guard studied him, then looked at Jennifer Brookbaine and Jim Wiley. "I assumed you were either another private eye, or a friend of his."

The lieutenant reached into a pocket, located his detectives badge, and dangled it from its leather pouch a few inches from the guards nose.

"Does this help?"

The guard glanced at the badge as though it

might have carried some, but not a lot of influence. "Oh . . ."

"Oh," Lindsay repeated. He hung the badge and its pouch from an outside vest pocket on his coat, then pulled his thirty-eight revolver from its holster. Flipping it open, he emptied the spent shell casings left over from his unsuccessful battle with the Mercedes into the palm of his hand, dropped them into a free pocket, then began inserting fresh cartridges.

The gun carried more influence than the badge. Like a cobra staring at a flute, the guard's eyes began to follow the slowly wavering weapon. "Oh," he said again, this time with a touch of respect and more than a touch of apprehensive concern.

When the last bullet was loaded, Lindsay flung the cylinder shut with a little more force than was necessary. The click of metal hitting metal and then metal connecting with leather as the weapon was slapped back into its holster caused the guard to wince in his chair.

Purposely leaving the gun conspicuously visible, he flipped open his wrinkled pad and poised his pen as if fully expecting a confession. Hearing none forthcoming, he reached deep within himself and brought up the warmest most disarming tone of voice a crotchety old policeman such as himself could muster.

"Now you son of a bitch, did you, or did you not, see the person who ran past you?"

Any dreams the guard was having about the lady in the centerfold and an easy interrogation by an officer of the law who was hampered by his police department's rules of public etiquette, began to disappear.

"No. Yes. I saw him, but I don't know who he was."

"I know, you know," Lindsay insisted, having found the soothing good-cop voice he had thought about using a moment earlier. You also know these questions will be a lot easier to answer for me now than they're going to be when I have you driven downtown by uniformed police officers, in a clearly marked squad car, lights a blazing, parked squarely in front of the precinct, and escorted past your friends who. . ."

Lindsay took a breath while he looked at his watch. "Who, I'm sure will be gathering in the precinct at this time of night, waiting to be processed for something or other, probably narcotics. And they will just as surely notice me nodding at everything you say, like you're the most cooperative witness I've ever brought in for questioning."

Another breath. "Whether you are, or whether you aren't."

"We could leave right now," he offered when there was still some hesitation, "although it could be kind of busy this time of night. We might have to wait at the front desk for a while until your friends are processed."

He straightened his badge a little to make sure he had the guards attention. "But don't you worry, I'll stay right there beside you for the entire time so that your friends will know you're safe with me."

The guard stared at the badge that had inched closer to his face, and the handle of the thirty-eight which had grown longer and larger as it pushed its way out from under Lindsay's coat. His previous unworried demeanor was beginning to show some cracks.

"Now, once more," Lindsay said. "Did you, or did you not, see the person who ran past your guard station?"

"I don't know. Maybe. I think so."

The guard pointed a finger at Jennifer. "She said that two other men were taken down to the precinct for interrogation, and then they disappeared. She said the police found them out in the desert, full of bullet holes."

"Don't be ridiculous," Lindsay replied. "We don't know yet that they were . . . full of bullet holes. Are you sure you don't know the person who came in tonight with Linda Barnes?"

"No. Yes, I saw him. I got a look at him too. A cowboy type person. But I didn't know him."

Increasing nervousness in the guard's answers indicated otherwise to Lindsay. "I believe I sense a little fear in your voice. When we were going into the building, you telephoned to let the person inside know we were coming. Why was that?"

"I don't know why. I just know that Lennie always told me to let him know if someone was coming."

"Lennie?"

"What?"

"Lennie. You identified the person who arrived with Ms. Barnes as Lennie."

"No, no I didn't."

"Yes, yes you did. Lennie who?"

The guard was quiet again.

"Are you afraid of Lennie?"

"No."

"Then why are you stammering?"

"I'm, I'm not stammering."

"Yes, you are stammering. The question is, why. And why are you so hesitant to answer my questions. Do you know what we call someone down at the precinct who hesitates before answering a question?"

"No . . ."

"We call him a person of interest who is

hiding something that he would like to get off his conscience."

To accentuate his point, Lindsay motioned with a thumb toward the ambulance that was waiting outside the office building. "We also call him a prime suspect who might have abetted in an attempted murder, or possibly even a murder."

The guard's eyes followed the lieutenant's outstretched thumb. He had seen the paramedics rush into the office structure with the gurney and wondered why. Beads of sweat began to appear on his forehead.

"Murder??!!"

"Murder. You do know that when you called Lenny to let him know we were coming, you were abetting. You also know that in court you could be considered as guilty as he is."

"He shot her! He shot his own sister?!"

"Shot her. Squarely in the back, just like the low down sniveling coward is going to shoot you in the back when he doesn't need you anymore. Now, are you sure you wouldn't like to confirm the last name of the person who arrived with Linda, who you have already identified as her brother."

Wavering, the guard began to stumble over his words. "Barnes," he finally blurted. "He was Lennie Barnes, Linda Barnes' brother."

"Now that wasn't so hard," Lindsay said. "Do you know Lennie Barnes personally?"

"Honest, I don't know him personally. I just know that he comes in all the time with Linda."

"All the time?"

"Quite often. He needs her clearance to get into the building."

"When?"

"Late at night."

"Like tonight?"

"Yes."

"What does he do when he comes in?"

"Sometimes he just goes in with her. I don't know what he's doing. Sometimes he picks up cartons of computers."

"With what? What was he driving? The Mercedes?"

"Usually. Sometimes he drives a truck, like a moving truck. He throws the cartons into the back, like he doesn't care about them."

"Like he doesn't care?"

"That's how it seemed to me."

"Was there a name on the truck?"

"Sandstorm, something or other."

"Did you say, Sandstorm?"

"Yes."

"And you never questioned him about what he was doing with the computers?"

"I don't question Lennie Barnes. All I know

is, he comes in with his sister, he tells me to let him know if anyone is coming, and he picks up computers. I don't ask why, he doesn't tell me why, and I don't care why. I still don't care why."

"So you are afraid of Lennie."

"Wouldn't you be?"

Lindsay didn't answer. Smiling a crooked smile to himself, he looked back at the heap of wrecked vehicles he had just climbed down from. Deciding the guard might be more valuable right where he was than in a jail cell, or full of bullet holes out in the desert, he stared into his eyes and asked in a tone that was mostly a demand. "You're not planning to leave town, are you?"

Sensing a possible reprieve, the guard stammered, "No. No, no, no, of course not."

"Good," Lindsay said. "Now, for your own safety, do not tell anyone that you and I had this conversation, and unless you've left something out, I'll try to forget it too. Are you okay with that?"

Accepting the guard's nod as an answer, Lindsay left him with his magazine, and like the other four or five or six, he had lost count, witnesses he let go that evening, he hoped his latest suspect would still be around in the morning.

With Jennifer and Jim beside him, he walked toward the office building. The reception area seemed quieter and more somber than it had when they arrived earlier, even though nothing had changed in the foyer. They took the elevator to the fourth floor and were met by paramedics pushing a gurney toward them from the direction of the cubicle where he had discovered the wounded woman.

"Linda Barnes?" he asked as they passed.

"I'm afraid so," one of the medics answered. "She's in bad shape, but still alive. The bullet appears to have missed vital organs."

"I hope you make it," Lindsay said softly, then he proceeded to the area where Lorraine had been comforting Linda Barnes until the paramedics arrived. The contents of Linda's purse were strewn around her desk.

"It was like this when we arrived," Lorraine said. "It looks like whoever shot her was looking for something. Most of her files have been scattered around, as though someone was searching for something specific."

"He missed some of them," George said. "I discovered purchase orders at the back of a cabinet that had been misplaced or perhaps hidden by Ms. Barnes. It appears that names on checks and bank account numbers were altered so that payments were made to another company instead of the companies that actually provided the services."

"Whose name is on the purchase orders?" Lindsay asked. "Let me guess. Linda Barnes."

"Yes. And if my addition is correct, Wiley Electronics paid them more than fifty thousand dollars last month."

"And the name of the company on the altered checks?"

"Sandstorm Distribution."

"Like in Sandstorm Automotive and Used Car Sales downtown, Sandstorm Car Rentals at the airport, and a truck with Sandstorm written on the side that comes in here late at night, with Lennie Barnes driving. The security guard said that Lennie was picking up cartons of computers and throwing them into the truck, like he didn't care what happened to them."

"Throwing?"

"That's what the guard said. Any idea what that was about?"

"No. But it's interesting, since we also found a note that someone had sent to Linda, or perhaps Lennie, to let them know where certain computers could be found."

Jim examined the list and then handed it to the lieutenant. "We don't even sell some of these computers. They are mostly outdated or partially assembled stock that have been replaced by newer models. I can see why no one would miss them. What would Lennie Barnes want with outdated or partially finished computers?"

"I don't know about the computers," Lindsay replied, "but I recognize the address on the invoices. It's a mailing and shipping service on the other side of town. They rent mailboxes, except they don't call them post office boxes, they call them suites. A hundred other companies are using the same location as their business address."

"We didn't find anything else out of the ordinary," Lorraine said, "except a crumpled list of names that Linda had thrown into a garbage pail beside her desk."

"Anybody we know on it?"

"Just everybody in Wiley Electronics that is somebody, and has a job that Linda and Lennie might have been interested in. Jim's Regional Manager, Carl Rogers. Production Manager, John Wilson. Shipping Manager, Paul Cater. They've been invited to some kind of gala celebration and charity event at a large estate in a very exclusive area of the city, on Saturday evening."

"I'll ask about Linda Barnes and the list of names when I talk to Carl Rogers tomorrow," Jim said, "although it probably doesn't mean anything. Employees, especially managers, are often invited to business or social events."

George smiled. "There is also one name on the list who isn't an employee of Wiley Electronics that might be of interest to everybody."

"Oh? Who?"

"Lieutenant Raymond Lindsay of the Westland Police Department."

ELEVEN

Jim was not looking forward to confronting Carl Rogers about his relationship with Linda Barnes.

The letter of recommendation the manager had given Linda for the position in accounting didn't necessarily mean anything. He might have known her work history from another company and considered her the most qualified for the job, or he might have interviewed her and made the final decision in hiring her. But Jim had to ask anyway, even though he was not expecting it to be a pleasant experience.

He was sure his other appointment would be more enjoyable, and was looking forward to meeting Jennifer Brookbaine again. He had never met a female private investigator, and had not given any thought to a woman being in that profession. To him, private investigation was something that would be more suitable for a man, with sneaking down dark alleys, peeking through motel windows, and prying into people's personal lives.

On second thought, he thought, maybe a woman would be good at it.

He pulled George Brensley's latest Buick, which hadn't been blown up or shot full of holes, yet, into a parking lot and walked the short distance to a stately, early nineteenth century office building.

Most of the suites in the building still had the original wide oak entrances, with engraved bronze plaques and expensive furniture inside that spelled out the success of high priced Westland law firms and other upscale white collar businesses.

Somewhere along a hallway, the expensive entrances came to an end and a single oak door that might have been more at home in the original building appeared. On a frosted glass window, Haddel and Brookbaine Investigations, was inscribed.

Letting his imagination drift to a nineteen-forties black and white mystery movie he had seen on television, he half expected a craggy old investigator with his feet on a desk or an office clerk chewing gum and filing her nails, like one might find in the same movie.

Instead, Jennifer was sitting behind a modern lawyer type desk similar to the ones he had been given a glimpse of as he walked down the hallway. She lifted her eyes from some paperwork, peered over her reading glasses, and gave him a welcoming smile.

"Good morning," she said. "I hope you don't find our historical building a little too quiet after yesterday's excitement."

"It's a nice change," Jim replied, happy that she wasn't the clerk filing her nails or the crusty old investigator with his feet on a desk. "Your sign says Haddel and Brookbaine."

"Harry Haddel, my partner. The sign used to say, Haddel Investigations. That was when I attended Westland University and Harry gave me a job working part time for him. He paid for most of my education and I've been with him ever since."

"How come I never saw you at Westland?"

"Separate paths, I guess. You were probably preparing to take on the world with your business and electronics and marketing classes, and I, without even knowing it, was preparing to take on wayward spouses and white collar criminals, with psychology and psychiatry and studying the human mind. As it turned out, we were both right. You used yours to build a world wide company, and with Harry's mentoring, I used mine in figuring out why people do the things they do."

"And have you figured out why people do the things they do?"

"Some. Some, we'll never know. They just do them."

"Your office is different from the other offices."

"The style? Oh, that's Harry. The doorway was there when his father opened the office ninety or so years ago. Harry couldn't bear to remove it when his father retired, so he kept it for sentimental reasons. Same with his furniture. It belonged to his father. You probably noticed, many of the other offices are lawyers. The original tenants used Harry's father's services, their son's and daughters used Harry's services, and their sons and daughters use Harry's and my services. They hire us to keep track of whatever it might be that they want to keep track of. I also get to use their services when I overstep the law a wee bit."

"A wee bit?"

"Like pretending to be a hooker to get evidence, and finding myself in jail with Lorraine giving me advice on how to get out. I still do it occasionally. You might have noticed my red dress last night."

"I was hoping that was for me."

"You never know. I wear it for other occasions too. Lorraine says if I ever lose my job, I could have another occupation to fall back on."

Jim's collar was feeling tighter than it had a moment earlier. "How did you get your name on the door?" he asked, deciding to change the subject.

"Easier than you might think. One night, during a long stakeout, Harry became melancholy and asked if I would like to become his partner. I said, how much. He said, how about two beers. And as luck would have it, I happened to have enough money on me for two beers. So here I am. Who could turn down a partnership with the greatest private eye in the world for two beers."

"It sounds like Harry is a very special person to you."

"Yep. He's a great friend and he taught me just about everything I know, in and out of the business. Once when I was dating in college, he even tried to help me with the facts of life."

"A little late, wasn't he?"

"A little, but his heart was in the right place."

"How did he do?"

"Not bad. He missed out a few things, but I'm not sure they even had some of them when he was in college."

Jim looked around the office. Except for Jennifer's desk and surrounding fixtures, most of the furnishings, including a desk that appeared to be as original as the door, would have been right at home in the nineteen-fifties.

"Harry's?" he asked.

"Yes. He's out doing a little investigating right now. I mentioned the problems your company is having and he offered to look into it for me. He found that Sandstorm Distribution, Sandstorm Auto Rentals, and Sandstorm Used Car Sales are all owned by the same person, a man by the name of Jerry Whittnor."

"Interesting connection."

"Whittnor also owns a trucking company with terminals here and across the border in Mexico. Their trucks go back and forth quite often and they sometimes carry shipments of computers and other electrical components that your company might use."

"If Whittnor is involved in what's been going on, he doesn't appear to be covering his tracks very well. His companies are popping up all over the place."

"Harry said the same thing. He believes that Lennie Barnes, with the help of his sister and maybe the security guard in your parking lot, could be carrying out something on their own at Wiley Electronics, in addition to writing checks to themselves for goods never received, and stealing worthless computers."

"Such as?"

"Who knows. Drugs? That's the only occupation I'm aware of that Barnes is involved in. Throw in Whittnor's trucks going back and forth across the border and you could have a recipe for drug trafficking."

"Except Lieutenant Lindsay believes an international crime family could be in on the deal. And I somehow doubt that they would approve of the stupid things that Barnes and his sister are doing on their own."

"I doubt it too," Jennifer said, "and if they aren't aware of it, I would hate to be in Barnes shoes when they find out. He would have to be crazy to use their trucks and limos for his own criminal activities."

"We'll find out. Are you ready to go back to Wiley Electronics and do some troubleshooting? Lorraine said I'd better get over here and hire you, before you accepted another job."

Jennifer laughed. "That was nice of her, especially since I don't have another job waiting for me. Besides, I've already decided you're going to hire me. I started working on your case last night and Harry and I have both been working on it today for the past three and a half hours."

Jennifer stood and moved from behind her desk. Her hair swirled around her shoulders and her high heels, skirt and blouse, which might have been meant to camouflage her figure, only seemed to accentuate it.

Jim could feel his emotions overtaking his

reason for the visit. He couldn't help smiling in admiration. Not missing his interest, Jennifer smiled back.

"Heels and dresses often get me a lot more information than pants and flats and my skills as an investigator," she explained. "But just in case my feminine charms don't work, I keep a pair of running shoes in the car."

Not finding words to express his feelings, Jim could only smile again in agreement.

As they drove toward Wiley Electronics, he glanced across the car at the beautiful private investigator that Lorraine and George Brensley had brought into his life. She was a mystery he wanted to get to know better, and hopefully as she carried out her investigation, they would be seeing a lot more of each other.

His visit to Westland was beginning to look a lot more interesting.

TWELVE

John Wilson was waiting for them in the production office at Wiley Electronics. He had been plant manager for many years, enjoyed his job, and was good at it. Jim had offered him promotions on several occasions but he declined, preferring to remain in the assembly and manufacturing areas. The company would be hard pressed to find a replacement who could do the job as well. However, Jim let him know the offer was always open.

It was Wilson who discovered money was being embezzled from the company. He had not known where the profits were going, he just knew there should have been more of them, considering the amount of computers and other products the plant was turning out. Like George Brensley, he met a brick wall at the regional managers office when he attempted to investigate.

"Let me show you around," he said to Jennifer, motioning toward a new line of computers that were in the process of being assembled.

Most of the employees remembered Jim. He was a popular boss when he managed the operation. "Are you back to stay?" one of them asked.

Angelina Bales had been with the company since the days when Jim's father ran the operation, before they had gone international and before Jim moved to New York. She had begun as a production worker and quickly demonstrated skills that allowed her to work her way up to quality control supervisor and head electronics technician. Like John Wilson, she was offered a promotion on several occasions but declined, preferring to stay in the job she enjoyed.

"You never know, Angelina," Jim answered. "Westland is one of my favorite places. Do you have a position in production for me?"

The technician laughed. "No, but I know where you can get one. Upstairs. It sure would be nice to have you back again." She studied Jennifer. "Someone new in the company?"

"This is Jennifer Brookbaine," Jim said. "She's a private investigator who will be doing some work for us."

"Does this have anything to do with the lady who was shot in the purchasing department?" Angelina asked.

"I'm afraid so," Jim replied, wondering how she knew about the shooting.

"The grapevine," she answered. "Probably

everyone in the company has heard about it by now."

"What are you repairing?" Jennifer inquired. She pointed to some parts on a shelf. "And what are those? I don't get to see the insides of computers very often."

"Power supplies, printed circuit boards, communication software, just about anything that can go wrong in a computer. Right now I'm waiting for parts we've ordered so I can go ahead and repair them."

"We know about the shortage of parts," Jim said. "John and I are going upstairs to see Carl and get it straightened out."

In his office, Carl Rogers rose from behind his desk to greet them. "Jim, how are you?"

A touch of coolness crept into his voice as he addressed Wilson. "John."

"Carl," Wilson responded.

"It's nice to see you," Jim said, shaking Roger's hand. "How is everything going?"

"Not bad. I guess John told you about our problem. We both agree that profits are disappearing. The only difference is, he thinks they're disappearing up here and I think they're going off the shipping dock."

"In what way?" Jim asked.

"One for the customer and one for the black market." The regional manager looked at

Wilson. "Computers aren't very difficult to unload, you know."

"That's bullshit," Wilson shot back. "We can account for every computer that came off the assembly line and went out of the shipping department."

The older man was getting red. "And what about parts? You order twice as many parts as the assembly area needs. You tell me where all those parts are going if not into computers and out the door."

"We're not getting parts," Wilson responded, his voice rising slightly. "Your purchasing department is paying for them but we're not getting any."

Jim interrupted their disagreement. "Let's sit down and talk this over. And maybe we can discover what is really going on."

He introduced Jennifer to Rogers, then told him about the investigation the night before, finding Linda Barnes fighting for her life in the purchasing department, and discovering the invoices and parts orders that had been altered in the embezzlement.

"I'd like to see if you can shed some light on Linda," Jim said. "We think it might be forged, but we found a letter of recommendation with your name on it, in her purse."

"I didn't write her a recommendation for

anything," Rogers said, "although I did interview her and couldn't find any reason not to give her the job. But the final decision was made by someone in the purchasing department."

"What about the letter?" Wilson pressed.

"I don't know. I just know it wasn't me. What difference does it make anyway?"

Jim told the two men about Sandstorm Distribution and the electronics orders Linda Barnes had issued, for which they had paid fifty thousand dollars but had never received anything.

"Son of a bitch," Rogers muttered. "Right here under our noses. I guess I owe you an apology, John. Maybe now that we've found where the money is going, we can start making some profits again."

"There's a little more to it than that," Jim said. "That was only fifty thousand. There appears to be a lot more."

"At least," Wilson added. "I don't have to be a chief executive to add up a profit and loss statement."

The regional manager's face was getting red again. "Are you accusing me?"

"I'm not accusing anybody," Wilson said, "but we've just stopped a small leak. There could be a whole flood out there."

Jim interrupted again. "Carl, we don't know where the problem is but we're going to need your help if we're to find it. Jennifer and I will be checking invoices, purchase orders, and any other paperwork that flows between accounting and purchasing, the plant, and outside vendors, but you've been here longer and know more about this place than anybody. Will you give us a hand?"

"Anything you need," Rogers said. "Just ask for it. I'll start by telling each department that you're conducting an audit. We do it every once in a while anyway, so there shouldn't be any problem."

They left the regional manager in his office and headed toward the shipping area. The shipping supervisor met them as they were coming in the door.

Paul Cater extended his hand and shook Jim's hand enthusiastically. "Nice to see you again. What brings you to these parts?"

"We're doing a little troubleshooting," Jim replied. "This is Jennifer Brookbaine. You might have heard, a lady was shot in the accounting department last night, and she has been hired to investigate."

"We want to talk to you about shipping procedures," Wilson said. "It seems that we have some money disappearing and we just want to make sure none of it is going out on the trucks."

"I'm sure it hasn't," Cater replied. "We can account for every computer and everything else that has been shipped. But I suppose anything is possible. As fast as a person can think up one way to stop theft, somebody else will think up another way. But we haven't had any trouble that we know of since those computers disappeared off the dock three years ago."

"What happened then?" Jennifer asked.

"It was the damnedest thing. A whole pallet full of them was there in the evening and gone the next morning. Nobody knew where. Three days later a truck driver asked one of the assembly line workers if he wanted to buy a computer. He didn't know that the guy worked for John."

"We told him that if he didn't talk, we were going to prosecute him alone for the entire theft," Wilson said. "He spilled his guts. There were five of them, the truck driver, a security guard, two dock workers and the shipping supervisor."

Jennifer looked at Cater.

Wilson laughed. "Not this supervisor. Paul replaced him. If it hadn't been for that truck driver needing beer money, we might never have caught them."

"I remember it," Jim said. "Are they still locked up?"

"A couple are. As far as I know, the others plea bargained or got lighter sentences. They're probably out by now and working for some other company. I'm just glad they don't work for us."

With assurances that they could have all the freedom they needed to investigate shipping procedures, they left Cater and Wilson and walked to the parking lot.

"Would you like to see where Lennie Barnes lives," Jennifer asked as Jim turned onto the street. "I think you might be impressed by his neighborhood."

She directed him to an exclusive high-priced area where years earlier wealthy families, wanting to escape the busy downtown area, had moved and built private estates. Most of the properties were the size of large farm fields and measured in acres. At the time they were built, the properties were out in the country, but since then they had gradually been surrounded by the sprawl of the city.

"Lennie Barnes owns this?" Jim exclaimed as they stopped at one of the estates.

"It's in his name," Jennifer replied. "Although Harry believes that someone else really owns it. Maybe Whittnor, or whoever

Whittnor reports to.   It supposedly has a mortgage on it for more than it's worth, and a life insurance policy on Lennie for even more than that."

"That doesn't bode well for Lennie. If I were in his shoes, I'd be watching my back for the people in line to collect on the policy."

Whoever owned the property had kept their privacy by erecting a high grated fence around the perimeter.   Each bar was topped with a dagger shaped ornament that was meant to be partly decorative and partly to keep the public out. Along the fence, thick shrubbery had been planted and trimmed to the same height. If the daggers and the shrubs didn't keep intruders at bay, the thorns and their allergies probably would do the job.

The gate at the entrance was the same design as the fence, except it was curved up in the center where its two sections met.   Lamps adorned concrete pillars on either side and an intercom jutted out from a stake in the ground. On a separate post, higher than the others, a camera kept watch over vehicles that entered or left.

There was not much to see of the main house. It was mainly hidden by the foliage along the fence and trees scattered around the yard. The roof was visible. It had chimneys that contained two or three stacks each, indicating the quantity of fireplaces, and eave-covered windows announcing the amount of rooms on the top floor.

A driveway curved and disappeared soon after leaving the entrance, and was not seen again. The only evidence of where it might have gone was the top of a delivery vehicle that appeared from somewhere at the rear of the property.

As they waited, a large truck like the kind companies used around the city to make deliveries, exited and turned onto the street.

The vehicle wasn't unusual in itself except for the company identification painted on the side, and a driver that Jennifer recognized.

"Sandstorm Distribution," she exclaimed. "And Lennie Barnes."

THIRTEEN

"For a company we never heard of, can't locate, has a mail drop box for an address, and its only business appears to be stealing money and computers from Wiley Electronics late at night, Sandstorm Distribution certainly gets around a lot," Jennifer said as the truck passed.

Jim had already pressed his foot down on the Buick's accelerator. He fell in a block behind the truck and kept pace. "And we're going to find out where it gets around to," he replied. "Starting right now. I say we follow Mister Lennie Barnes and see where he leads us."

Barnes headed in the direction of Wiley Electronics. He slowed down as he passed the entrance to the shipping department, then sped up and hurried away. He merged onto a freeway, drove for several miles, then turned off and entered the parking lot of a dingy motel.

The motel was attached to an even more dingy bar. Both businesses appeared quiet except for partially lit neon signs announcing the services they offered, and a few overhead lights flickering on and off, announcing the approach of sunset and evening.

"I'm familiar with this place," Jennifer said. "It's a handy hideaway for men to have a few drinks, meet ladies of the evening, or carry out clandestine activities such as sales and purchases they don't want the law to know about. Husbands who want to get away from their wives, and the occasional wife who wants to get away from her husband, also come with their dates to while away the evening."

"While . . . away?"

"Yes. While away." Jennifer bent a thumb in the direction of the motel. "Sometimes they while away the entire night."

Jim looked around the neighborhood. It consisted of mostly older run down properties and factories that had seen better days, and without the neon signs and half-lit street lights, were even darker than the bar and motel.

"In this place?"

"Where would you suggest they go? The Waldorf?"

"As a matter of fact, I would. You've been here, at night, by yourself?"

"A few times. It's sometimes part of the job. But don't worry. I'm not always alone."

In answer to Jim's inquisitive gaze, she explained. "In a place like this, a couple is less conspicuous than a single woman, unless she happens to be one of the ladies I mentioned. So

Harry is usually with me. He becomes my boss or an older gentleman friend and I become his Moll."

"Moll?"

"Did I mention that Harry lives a little bit in the past. Anyway, we fit in very well with all the other wayward men and their love interests."

"What else do they do in there?"

"Dance. Harry calls it foreplay, before they go to the motel to while away the rest of the night."

Barnes had gone inside the bar for a few minutes, then exited. He wasn't alone. Two other men were with him.

"I recognize those men," Jim said. "They used to work for Wiley Electronics, and were part of the gang that stole the pallet of computers off the shipping dock three years ago. Which means they probably know the layout of our building, and where computers are located."

"Frank Ellis and Pete Salter," Jennifer replied. "I recognize them from somewhere else. Along with Barnes, they both sell drugs on the street. I also saw Ellis in court a couple years ago, charged with smuggling of some kind, probably drugs. His arrest sheet is as long as your arm, and usually he gets off. Somebody makes sure he gets only the best lawyers, probably the same ones that keep getting Lennie Barnes off. So far, the police have had a difficult time coming up with another case against him."

The Sandstorm Distribution truck, with Barnes and his two cohorts, exited the parking lot, drove farther into the industrial area, then turned into another street and disappeared from view.

Jim was about to accelerate to keep it in sight when another truck, a tractor trailer, came from the opposite direction. It turned into the same street and followed closely behind the Sandstorm truck.

"A Whittnor Transportation truck," Jennifer exclaimed. "The same people who own all of the Sandstorm companies."

They were about to follow when Jim braked to a stop. "I've been in this area," he said, "and that street might be a dead end. Let's take a look before we drive in somewhere we can't get out of."

The street came to a stop at a high metal gate that blocked the entrance to a property that was difficult to see into. Although the entrance appeared new, the area behind it was in disrepair. The gate had been opened to allow the Sandstorm truck and the Whittnor

Transportation trailer to pass through, then closed again.

"George and I played around here when we were kids," Jim said. "That used to be a junkyard where we came to get parts for our bicycles. The old couple who owned it let us have anything we could find. Whoever owns it now doesn't seem so friendly, and they must have moved the entrance. It used to be around the corner on the other side, and the gate was always open."

"You don't suppose that entrance is still there?"

"We can take a look. It's either that or go in this entrance. And if these are the same guys who tried to kill us, it might not be the wisest thing to walk up and say hello, here we are."

They followed the fence around a corner and to a narrow street where Jim and George had ridden their bicycles and played with other children. The area had changed, and not for the better. Properties they remembered as relatively well kept with friendly people, were now old, mostly dilapidated, vacant, and strewn with garbage.

A discarded sofa that someone had dumped against the fence was partially hiding a wooden gate that had once served as the entrance to the junkyard, but now, having been unused for many years, was missing boards, and decaying from disrepair.

Without speaking, Jim picked up a piece of discarded bed frame, forced it into one of the openings and pried. The tired wood and the rusted nails that held the boards together creaked and moaned as they slowly gave way to the iron.

They hesitated to make sure they had not been detected. Then not waiting for Jim to make the first move, Jennifer took the piece of iron out of his hands, set it on the ground, hiked her skirt, bent a leg through the hole he had just made, and motioned for him to follow.

The narrow drive that Jim and George had used to enter when they were kids was still there, although it was overrun with weeds. It was obvious that children were no longer visiting to play out their fantasies and find parts for their bicycles.

They passed rows of scrapped cars, piled three or four high, and piles of compressed metal which were once automobiles, before they met their fate in the giant compactor the present scrap yard now used. On the other side of the property, backed into a shipping dock, the Sandstorm Distribution truck and the Whittnor Transportation trailer were parked.

The narrow path took them to an area

behind an old building that had once served as the office for the junkyard. It was apparently still in use. Jim and Jennifer crept to the side of the building, and in the shadows, each placed an ear close to the thin wall.

Faint outlines of several people could be seen through the dirty windows, and muffled voices could be heard. The angry voice of one of the men was rising above the others.

"Did you talk to your contact in the shipping department?" he asked one of the men.

The second voice belonged to Lennie Barnes. "No. I tried to, but it looked like there's some kind of investigation going on, and the security guard has been replaced. I didn't think I should go near it."

Seeming to accept Barnes' omission of his activities the night before, his theft of computers, the attempted murder of his sister, pushing Lieutenant Lindsay's squad car up a pile of wrecked vehicles, being the reason the security guard was no longer on duty, and causing the investigation that prevented him from seeing his contact at Wiley Electronics, the angry man spoke again.

"Don't worry about the security guard. I've arranged for him to be back on duty tomorrow night. As for you, you just look after the exchange. You've got to get in there."

Whatever the message, Barnes apparently didn't get it all. "We will," he said. "We just need to lie low for a while."

"We can't lie low," the other man yelled. "And if we don't make that trade by tomorrow night, you won't have to worry about making any more deliveries, because somebody's ass is going to be feeding coyotes out in the desert, and it isn't going to be mine."

Barnes consented, sounding resigned to doing the job even though he was opposed. "But I'm going to need some help."

"You'll get your help," the man in charge answered. "Ellis and Salter will be going with you."

Frank Ellis spoke for the first time. "Is the exchange going to be the same place as last time?"

The building was quiet, then the man in charge spoke again. "You'll find out tomorrow night. How much have you been talking?" A threat was in his voice. "You're going to have to learn to keep your mouth shut."

A door on the building was opened and slammed shut, and two men could be seen walking through the semidarkness of twilight toward the Sandstorm truck. The engine started, the whir of the gate opening and closing could be heard at the property entrance, then the area was quiet again. When the conversation inside the building continued, the angry man and Lennie Barnes were no longer present.

"Something big is happening," Ellis said. "I overheard Charlie York talking to someone on the telephone, about an important shipment that's coming in tomorrow night. I got the impression that whatever it is, will be exchanged for something that's coming in from somewhere in the east."

"Any mention about what the two shipments are?" Salter asked.

"They didn't say, but taking into account that Lennie is involved, one of them is probably from Mexico, and probably drugs."

"And the other one?"

"I don't know. Money, maybe. I got the impression there was a lot of money involved, more that what they would get from a few stolen computers. I know what I'm going to do with my share. I'm getting the hell out of town, maybe out of the state."

"Do you think Charlie York knew that Lennie was lying to him about what he was doing at Wiley Electronics last night?"

"He must. I heard him on the telephone, talking to someone. Lennie's name came up a couple times, and not in a good way. If he's smart, he'll also get out of town. And if you and I are smart, we'll be heading in the opposite direction."

Jennifer and Jim had been listening intently at the wall and failed to notice a movement at the corner of the building. It wasn't until they heard a low growl that either of them reacted.

They looked up to see a dog baring its teeth at them. The animal was large, the size of a Labrador Retriever, except it had what appeared to be the head of a Schnauzer and the tail of an unshorn sheepdog. They couldn't tell exactly what other breeds might be present in the animal, but it looked like it would have no trouble tearing them apart.

"Why didn't you mention they had a guard dog here?" Jennifer asked.

"Because they didn't have a guard dog the last time I was here?"

"Are you sure?"

Jim stared at the dog and winced. "I would have remembered that. What we need is something we can use to distract him, besides us?"

Jennifer felt around in her handbag. "Some gum."

Jim shrugged his shoulders. "Give it to him. It's better than sitting here while he works up an appetite."

Moving as slowly as she could, Jennifer lifted the package of gum from her handbag. "What if he doesn't like it?" she said, offering a stick to the inquisitive dog.

Jim was quiet, except his head leaned a little sideways and his eyes shifted toward her purse where the handle of her thirty-eight revolver had become visible.

Jennifer put her hand on the gun. "Oh no you don't. I'll shoot the crooks inside the building if you want me to, but I'm not shooting any dogs."

She let her words hang in the air for Jim to decide what she thought about people and dogs.

He stared at her, and then at the animal that was sniffing the gum in her hand. It relaxed for a moment, then gobbled it up and began chewing.

A second later the gum was gone and the dog looked into Jennifer's face, expecting another piece. She gave it to him.

"Come on," Jim whispered. "Let's get out of here while he's distracted."

At their first movement, the dog stopped and bared its teeth again. Its "Rrrrrr," wasn't so much a growl as it was a demand to know what they were doing there.

"More gum?" Jennifer offered.

"Brutus. Here Brutus."

The dog's ears stiffened at the sound of its name.

"Here Brutus," the man in the building called out again.

The dog looked at Jim and Jennifer one more time, then turned and disappeared around the corner.

Neither of them spoke as they ran to the path they had used to enter the junkyard. At the fence, they stopped and listened for sounds of anyone, man or beast, that might be following. They heard the hoarse voice of the man in the building.

"Who the hell's been feeding gum to the dog? Kids! Sic 'em Brutus!"

Jennifer and Jim could hear Brutus bounding between the piles of junk as they crawled through the opening in the fence to safety. They had just moved the wood and sofa back into position when the dog arrived. They stood panting on the outside while the animal stood on the inside, curiously watching them through the cracks.

"Rrrrrr," he grumbled again, as though asking what they were doing there.

"None of your business what we were doing here," Jennifer replied.

FOURTEEN

"Wiley Electronics."

"Where else could the exchange be?" Jim said, "If they're feeling as much heat as the men at the junkyard said they are, they're probably not going to use the junkyard or any other Whittnor property. The question is, what are they exchanging, what is coming in from Mexico, and what is coming in from the east coast."

"Probably drugs from Mexico," Jennifer answered. "I don't know about the east coast. Your guess would be as good as mine. I agree with you about your company being where the exchange will take place. Why else would Lennie Barnes be driving by the shipping department, and why else would Charlie York be asking if he made contact with someone."

"I don't suppose you're in the mood for a little late night investigation in the shipping department?" Jim asked.

"Of course I'm in the mood," Jennifer replied. "But first I have to go by my place and pick up someone who might assist in our investigation."

Jim drove to the neighborhood where

Jennifer lived and waited while she went into the house. When she reappeared a few minutes later, a black and white border collie was at her side.

"I'd like you to meet Sheeba," she said.

The dog jumped into the car and lay down with her rear end pressed against Jim. Her tail swished against his leg. The rest of her body stretched across the seat with her head nuzzled against Jennifer's thigh. After that she was still except for one eye that occasionally blinked open to examine the man that had come into her life.

"Nice to meet you, Sheeba," Jim said to his end of the dog. "I assume you are the someone who will be assisting our investigation."

"Yep," Jennifer answered. "She sometimes sees things and smells things that people don't notice."

"Like what? Sheep?"

"Funny. Drugs. Before I met her, Sheeba was in training to be a drug sniffing dog at the airport. She was doing very well too, until she failed a couple little tests."

"What kind of little tests?"

"Okay, big tests. She had some trouble with coffee beans. She couldn't detect drugs that smugglers buried in them. Maybe it was the caffeine, I don't know. Anyway, she can still detect drugs in other places, so she might be able to help us."

"What if there are drugs at our company, but they happen to be in a shipment of coffee?"

"Then we're on our own."

"What other tests did she fail?"

"She's apparently too friendly. Her trainer said she would rather play or be petted than work."

Jim put his hand on the end of the dog that seemed to enjoy being petted. "You could have fooled me."

"Not with people. With other dogs. She was more interested in playing than working. To make a long story short, she was tossed out of the program. So I got her."

"Anything else I need to know?"

"Maybe. I'll let her tell you herself, when we get to your shipping department."

Sheeba was quiet for most of the trip, only sitting up once and raising her head to sniff at a donut shop and let them know there was coffee in the air. After that she was quiet again.

A different security guard from the night before was on duty at Wiley Electronics. He recognized Jim, said hello, and waved them through. No one was working in the plant. In the glow of the few lights that were still burning, they made their way past the manufacturing area and to the shipping department.

Jim motioned toward an inventory of computer accessories and parts waiting to be transferred to the assembly area. "Look for anything out of the ordinary," he said. "Computers not wrapped, on a pallet, loose cartons laying around that look like they could be waiting for someone to pick up, unusual paper work, especially anything associated with Sandstorm Distribution."

Their conversation was interrupted by the sound of Sheeba barking. She had stayed beside Jennifer since they arrived, but now she was gone. There was no response when her name was called, except for a low growl at the front of an empty trailer.

Jim looked for her in the darkness. "Maybe we do have coffee beans," he quipped.

Jennifer ignored the comment. "Do you notice the name on the side of the trailer that Sheeba went into?"

"I noticed. Whittnor Transportation."

Jim joined Jennifer in the trailer where Sheeba was intermittently scratching the floor at the front and looking back to let Jennifer know she'd found something.

He ran his hands over the wood in the front wall. "Do you notice something strange about the sides on this trailer when you came in?" He asked.

"No, except the whole body looks like it has a double wall."

"That part is normal. The unusual part is the corners at the front. Outside, the corners are rounded. Inside, they're square. In order to do that, they would have to waste almost a foot of cargo space. Either they're trying to be neat, or there's something behind there."

Jennifer knocked on the front of the trailer, then knocked on the sides. They sounded slightly different. She ran her fingers along the corners, searching for anything that would provide a clue and a way to open it. Then she stopped.

"I've found it," she exclaimed.

A partially loosened screw had allowed a dust-covered latch to come loose and reveal itself. She found two remaining latches that were holding the panel in place. With help from Jim and a heavy tug, the wall swung outwards to reveal a hidden compartment.

It was empty.

Jim moved a finger back and forth, calculating the area and the amount of computers it would hold.

"Portable computers, I suppose a few," he said. "Larger desk top models, not many at all, especially if they're in cartons. No matter how I work it out, there aren't enough computers in our company to equal what this space would be worth full of drugs."

"I agree," Jennifer said. "Whatever it is, if this truck is going back and forth to Mexico, add in Lennie Barnes and his friends, a bought border agent to make it easier to get through customs, a crooked security guard outside your building, Charlie York, Jerry Whittnor, and whatever crime family they might be involved with, and you have the makings of a first class smuggling ring. I say we close it up, hope that their contact in Wiley Electronics doesn't notice we discovered it, and wait until tomorrow night for Barnes and his friends to make the exchange."

Against Sheeba's wishes, they closed the compartment, reset the latches, and did as much as they could to make the trailer appear that it hadn't been tampered with.

"Would you settle for a cookie?" Jennifer asked as she joined the dog, who was looking quite pleased with herself, at the rear of the trailer.

"Your assistant has certainly earned her cookie tonight," Jim said.

Jennifer was looking just as pleased. "And more. Now, what's our next step?"

Before she finished the question, both she, Jim, and possibly Sheeba, knew the answer.

It was time to let Lieutenant Lindsay of the Westland Police Department know what they had discovered at the junkyard, the hidden compartment in the trailer, and the exchange they suspected would take place at Wiley Electronics the following evening.

FIFTEEN

The vacant side street behind Wiley Electronics was in darkness when Lieutenant Lindsay arrived the following evening. The last shift of employees had finished their work and left the parking lot, so if there was going to be a transaction of drugs and whatever else Lennie Barnes was dealing in, it would probably be taking place.

The lieutenant and Jennifer acknowledged each other with nods. He peered past her as if expecting George and Lorraine Brensley, and seemed surprised that they weren't there. She peered past him as if looking for other police officers to back him up, and wasn't surprised when she didn't see any.

"We're not here to start a gunfight," Lindsay said, answering her silent question. "We're here to observe and report."

"Who all knows we're here?" he asked Jim.

"Just us," Jim replied.

"What about the security guard?"

"He's the same one you talked to when Linda Barnes was shot, but he won't see us. There's an emergency exit at this end of the building that he can't see from his station, and if he's as lazy as he appeared to be the last time we met, he won't be bothered. I deactivated the alarm so we can enter without him knowing."

They walked along the back of the building, entered through the emergency exit, and moved quietly through the plant to the shipping area where trucks were backed against the dock, waiting to be loaded with freight. Jim pointed out the Whittnor trailer with the hidden compartment and the large doorways that vehicles would probably come through if a trade was to be made.

Lindsay looked around, searching for possible concealment. "How often does the guard come around?" he asked.

"Every hour, but it shouldn't be difficult to avoid him."

The lieutenant pointed to a mezzanine high above the shipping floor that was piled high with cartons and other shipping supplies. "I want you two up there," he said, "for your own safety."

Then he motioned toward a darkened doorway that led to the production area. "Will the guard go in there?"

"No. He might go past it, but he won't bother looking there."

"Good. That's where I'll be. And unless you

hear from me, leave your guns in your holsters."

He paid additional attention to Jennifer. "And purses. And don't make a sound. Like I said, our job here is to see what they're up too, not get into a gun fight."

They took their positions and the building lapsed into silence, until the echo of a door opening and closing brought them to attention. The outline of the security guard was visible as he walked past. A few minutes later they heard another door open and close at the opposite end of the shipping dock and the building was quiet once more.

A quarter hour after the guard had made his first inspection, they heard the door open again. This time he didn't walk through, but instead moved to a wall near the shipping office and pressed a button on a control panel. The whir of an electric motor could be heard as one of the large shipping doors was wound overhead. At the same time, they could make out the rumble of a diesel engine outside.

Headlights of a tractor trailer cut across the open doorway, illuminating the walls inside. Then the driver swung the truck around and backed in. It came to a halt as the rear of the trailer slammed into bumpers along the edge of the shipping dock.

Closely behind, a smaller truck drove in through the same doorway. It swung around and reversed into the space left open between the two larger trailers. In the reflection of their headlights, the Sandstorm Distribution vehicle that Jim and Jennifer had followed the day before became visible.

The tractor trailer's engine vibrated to a stop and headlights were turned off, leaving the warehouse in semidarkness. Then the whir of the electric motor could be heard once more as the shipping door came down and stopped against the concrete.

In place of the trucks' headlights, overhead shipping lights on flexible arms were turned on and directed into the rear of the Sandstorm truck and the trailers on either side. Lennie Barnes, along with Frank Ellis and Pete Salter appeared out of the darkness.

"Let's get this shit exchanged and get the hell out of here," Barnes growled as he climbed onto the dock behind the trucks. "Somebody knows something is going on, and the less time we spend here the better."

The three men began carrying armfuls of cardboard containers from the Sandstorm truck to the hidden compartment in the Whittnor trailer. When that job was completed, they closed the compartment, moved to the newly arrived tractor trailer, and began transferring packages wrapped in tape from it to the empty Sandstorm truck.

"Is that it," Barnes asked as Frank Ellis delivered the last package to the Sandstorm truck?

"That's it," Ellis replied.

"Good," Barnes said, bringing the discussion abruptly to an end. He began to walk away, then pulled a gun from beneath his jacket, turned around, and shot Ellis three times.

As Ellis fell to the floor, Pete Salter stood motionless, stunned. Then he reached for his own gun. Before his could use it, Barnes shot him, the same way he had shot his comrade. Both men lay on the floor, not moving.

With Barnes shooting of his two accomplices, Lindsay disobeyed his own instructions to wait for a command. His voice boomed though the warehouse.

"Freeze!"

The building was quiet for a moment as Barnes searched the semidarkness behind the shipping lights, trying to determine who was there.

"Freeze!" Lindsay called out again. "This is the . . ."

Barnes didn't wait for further explanation. Gunfire blazed from the dock as he shot blindly at anything he thought might be a target, then he jumped to the shipping floor between the trucks.

The entire gunfight lasted only a few seconds, before the giant engine in the tractor trailer rumbled to life. Gears ground together as it jerked forward and smashed through the large shipping door, leaving the corrugated steel in splintered pieces.

Additional shots rang out as Barnes climbed into the smaller Sandstorm truck. It's engine struggled to start, then it too jerked forward, following the tractor trailer through the jagged hole that had been sliced through the door.

Jim and Jennifer joined Lindsay on the dock. As Jennifer kicked a gun beyond arm's reach of the two unmoving bodies, the lieutenant began walking toward what was left of the mangled shipping door. He did not appear to be in a hurry.

"Wait here and look after those two," he called back over his shoulder, "just in case they're still moving. And call for an ambulance, although I don't think it will be necessary. I'll be back." Then he disappeared into the darkness outside.

Jennifer didn't wait. Leaving Jim to guard the crime scene and the unmoving bodies, she disobeyed the lieutenant's order and ran after him. By the time they reached the security station, the two trucks had disappeared into the night.

"That way goes toward the junkyard," Jennifer said. "The other way goes toward the freeway and probably a faster get-a-way. If the police stakeout is in place at the junkyard, it should be covered."

"The tractor trailer took the freeway," Lindsay said. "The Sandstorm truck went in the other direction."

Jennifer looked up and down the deserted street. There was no sign of either truck. "How could you tell?" she asked.

"The copters told me."

"Copters?"

Lindsay pointed into the sky. "Helicopters. One is following the Sandstorm truck. The other is following the tractor trailer. According to a pilot, there is also one security guard running down the street like the devil, or perhaps Lennie Barnes, was after him."

"I didn't know we had two helicopters."

"We don't, but the F.B.I. and other federal agencies do. When I informed them about what you found, they offered to help out. They're as anxious to catch these guys as we are."

"We?"

"We. You, me, Wiley, along with the

helicopters and fifteen or sixteen unmarked cars, two officers each, keeping tabs on them. We aren't going to pick them up tonight. We want to see where they're going, then we want to see who their other contacts are."

Jim was waiting on the shipping dock. "I found what the exchange was," he informed them. "The tractor trailer that came in carried drugs, like Lieutenant Lindsay thought. That's what they were transferring to the Sandstorm Distribution truck."

He pointed to an area outside the doorway where the tractor trailer and the Sandstorm truck had broken through to escape. Nearby were several taped up plastic bags containing white powder that had spewed across the parking lot. "They lost some," he said. "It was spilled outside so I don't think Lennie got the rear door on the Sandstorm truck completely closed before he took off."

"And the exchange for the drugs? Any idea what the exchange was?"

"Part of it was money. I found a briefcase on the floor, full of hundred dollar bills. It was apparently payment for the drugs and was dropped during the shootout."

"What about the Whittnor trailer? What was being transferred to it from the Sandstorm truck?"

"Something I think you will be interested in," Jim replied as he led them into the Whittnor trailer. "Now we know what's worth more than computers. The hidden compartment was filled with semiautomatic weapons and cartons of ammunition."

"Somebody is going to be awfully angry when they show up without this trailer," Jennifer said, inspecting the arsenal.

"Maybe not," Lindsay answered. "The compartment was sealed up. So if a person didn't know where to look, we wouldn't have even known the guns were in there. They weren't planning to move it tonight or they would have brought another semi to pick it up. We'll empty it, seal it up again, and see if they're dumb enough to come back for it."

"Where do you think the guns were headed?" Jim asked. "Mexico?"

"Probably. They're more difficult to get over the border. Like drugs up here. Also, some of them might be finding their way to other countries. I'm not an expert on what goes on in the rest of the world. Right now, I'm having enough trouble trying to understand what's going on in Westland."

Lindsay eyed his two accomplices. "Any of your bullet casings lying around the shipping department?"

"No," Jennifer replied. "Like you said, we kept our guns in our holsters."

"Good," Lindsay answered. He pointed to the bodies of Frank Ellis and Pete Salter on the floor. "That will make it easier for me to explain the holes in these two. In the meantime, you can expect to be called as witnesses."

He smiled a crooked, almost friendly smile. "And you will have to explain how you uncovered this whole deal, starting with the bombings, shootings, chasing down leads in your company, discovering the connection to Sandstorm and tracing it to the junkyard. Then finding the hidden compartment in the trailer and being responsible for uncovering a crime ring that law enforcement, up until now, has been unable to locate."

Before either Jim or Jennifer could offer a comment, he added, "In the meantime, I'll track down our security guard and also see if Linda Barnes is awake. I suspect that both of them will be getting just about ready to sing like the proverbial canary to try and save their own necks."

The drive toward Jennifer's home afterwards seemed almost anticlimactic for Lindsay's two accomplices. After all the suspense and danger, ending with the gunfight in the shipping department and Lindsay's generous insistence that they take most of the credit for uncovering the crime ring, there didn't seem to be anything left for them to do.

Their part in the investigation of the theft of funds from Wiley Electronics appeared to be over. There was still someone in the company that the drug ring used as a contact who hadn't been apprehended, but hopefully when the security guard was picked up and Linda Barnes regained consciousness, they would shed light on who the person was.

The case had been solved, and yet there was no final solution. Other than the two men that lay dead on the shipping dock, no one had been apprehended. Jerry Whittnor, Charlie York, and Lennie Barnes were still on the loose and being tailed by the police. Most of the drugs were gone and probably stashed to be put into circulation when the heat was off. And Wiley Electronics had lost hundreds of thousands of dollars that would never be recovered.

"But with your help, we did stop the embezzlement," Jim said as he stopped the car in Jennifer's driveway. "And hopefully the police will prevent some of the drug trafficking."

Jennifer turned toward him. "Did I thank you for showing me a wonderful time this evening?"

"It wasn't bad for a second date, was it?" he answered. "I just don't know what I'm going to do to impress you next time."

She moved a little closer. "If you like, we could go on a real date tomorrow night. We could go out to dinner or a show or something. We could even leave our guns and Sheeba at home." Then she leaned across the car, put her arms around his neck and kissed him.

He held her in a long embrace. When her lips moved away from his, he looked into her eyes. "I thought investigators weren't supposed to date clients."

"I make exceptions," she whispered, leaning closer and kissing him again, "when I really, really like a client. I'll see you tomorrow."

"Nuts," Jim sighed, "I have to fly back to New York in the morning."

SIXTEEN

Lennie Barnes had not seen who was waiting in the darkness at the interrupted weapons for drugs exchange in Wiley Electronics' shipping department, but he was sure that, along with the Westland Police Department, Jim Wiley or George Brensley, or both had to be there.

Jim and George did not remember Lennie. But he remembered them, and he hated them. He had hated them since childhood when he saw them playing in the neighborhood around the junkyard with other children. To him, they represented everything he didn't have but wanted.

Lennie was a bully. Where others got into the occasional fistfight, he carried a knife and did not hesitate to use it. As he grew older and spent more time in the seedier areas of the city, he also carried a gun.

He committed his first murder when he was eighteen years old. When the clerk in a convenience store he held up was too slow in opening a cash register, he shot him. He used the small amount of money he got from the robbery to purchase drugs to sell on the street to addicts, or prospective addicts.

In the beginning, he was smart enough to stay away from drugs himself. But that didn't stop him from getting his friends, like Pete Salder and Frank Ellis addicted. Once they were hooked, he controlled them and used them to make deliveries for him.

Unfortunately for Lennie, he eventually gave in to the lure of the illicit products he sold. In the process, he became more irrational in his desperation to raise cash to feed his own increasingly expensive habit.

He even supplied the drugs to his sister that made her an addict. Linda Barnes was making an effort to straighten out her life and her dependency on her brother and his drugs when she managed to get a job in the purchasing department at Wiley Electronics.

She saw it as an incentive to work harder to give up her addiction. Lennie saw it another way. It was an opportunity to use her addiction, and her job, to his advantage. Like others who were under his control, he threatened to cut off her supply if she didn't co-operate.

At first, Linda provided a way into the company to steal computers. Then he realized she also had access to accounts payable, and ordered her to falsify purchase orders and other documents. Payments she made went to his own mail order drop in the name of Sandstorm Distribution, except Sandstorm never saw them. They went directly into his own pocket to make more purchases.

Just as Lennie controlled others, he was also controlled. The owner of the junkyard, Charlie York, was his boss. York in turn, took his orders from Jerry Whittnor of Whittnor Trucking.

As York reported to Whittnor, Whittnor reported to someone else, although Lennie was never told who. He was sure it was someone from out of state, since he had driven Whittnor and York to the airport on several occasions to pick up a limousine and to meet a flight from the east coast. The automobile was always rented in Barnes' name, but he was never allowed to see who they were meeting.

Whittnor and York ordered him to use the shipping department in Wiley Electronics for one reason only, the transfer of drugs for weapons and money. They did not authorize the after hours theft of computers or the embezzlement that he and his sister became involved in. Discovery by his superiors that he was stealing money for himself or using his own product, would mean death for him, and Linda.

There was plenty of money. The briefcase that was spilling hundred dollar bills around the shipping room floor at Wiley Electronics would be an important but small loss to the organization, but to Lennie it was cash he could use for himself if he could get his hands on some of it.   He made a try before a bullet from Lieutenant Lindsay's gun hit the Sandstorm truck near his head. Then he forgot about the money and raced out through the hole in the large shipping door the tractor trailer had made.

Lennie was also useful to the organization for other reasons. His name was on the deed to the estate where the Mayors Charity Ball was being held, although he was not allowed to spend much time there. It was used mostly to hold meetings with visiting leaders or to make connections in the community that the family could use to their advantage.

He was never told why his name was on the deed, but suspected it was to protect others higher up in the organization. With his name on the title, it would be difficult to make a connection between the estate and whoever paid for it. When he discovered it was mortgaged beyond its value and carried an insurance policy on his life for an even larger amount by a real estate holding company, whose name he didn't recognize, he began to worry.

The same applied to the Mercedes limo he

used for his own illegal purposes. It was always rented in his name to protect the identities of the higher ups who wanted it when they came to town. They knew Lennie used it for his own purposes in their absence, but allowed it. The limo, the house, and his life would be lost to him when he was no longer of value.

Lennie resented some jobs, like transporting drugs in the Sandstorm Distribution truck around Westland and other cities in the state. He considered the job beneath him, but he had no choice. He knew that if he didn't cooperate, his legal support would be withdrawn and he would probably go to prison the next time he was arrested.

He did enjoy other assignments, like planting the bomb in George Brensley's Buick. Word came down to Whittnor and York about the failed bombing attempt on Jim Wiley's car in New York, and when they heard about George Brensley asking questions in Wiley Electronics, he would also have to go.

Whittnor and York did not have anything against the two men personally. They just knew that their superiors wanted Wiley out of the way so they could gain control of Wiley Electronics and its connections around the world for their own purposes.

Barnes' unauthorized activities led to the

investigation by George Brensley. Whittnor and York did not know who George was, except he was snooping around in the Westland plant. They thought it might have something to do with their guns for drugs operation, when the investigation was really caused by the embezzlement that Barnes was involved in. Neither Jim nor George had any idea of what they had discovered, except that some money was missing.

Charlie York supplied the bomb for George's Buick at the airport. It took only a few seconds to install. While Linda stood watch, Lennie yanked the door lock and popped open the hood. He placed the bomb behind the motor so that the blast would travel back into the car's interior, then set it to go off a short time after it was activated by motion. He had completed the job and was walking away when he remembered that he had forgotten to set the timer.

York had told him about the attempt on Jim Wiley's life in New York and of the bombers being blown up themselves, so rather than risk his own life further, he sent his sister back to do the job. She had just finished when Jim and George exited an airport elevator and saw her hurrying away from the car.

Lennie had been told only to get rid of

George Brensley, and had not expected Wiley to be there. But he was quite happy to see him. "I'll get both of them with one blast," he informed his sister.

He had wanted to stay to see the explosion and the death of the men he hated, but after Linda was spotted, he could not afford to hang around. They got away from the area as quickly as possible, trying to run Wiley and Brensley down in the process.

When he heard the blast and saw the fireball, he returned, circled around the terminal, and watched from across the parking garage to see if the explosion had done its job. Instead, he saw Wiley and Brensley talking to the young man who hit George's Buick with his convertible and set off the bomb. He had considered going back to finish the job with bullets, until he saw the airport security guard walking toward them.

"Get rid of them," York screamed when he called with the news that the bomb had been discovered and the men were safe. "I don't care how you do it, just get rid of them."

Deciding it would be too dangerous to make another attempt that night, he disobeyed his superior's orders and instead went after another target for even more hateful reasons. He waited for Lorraine Brensley to leave her office, and then followed her and Jennifer for the ambush on the highway.

Linda drove while he prepared for the shootout. His first opportunity came when they pulled off the freeway onto the nearly deserted road that led to the foothills. He had planned to just drive up beside them and begin firing, but when the Mercedes was spotted and they took off, his task became more difficult.

It did not take long to narrow the gap between the powerful Mercedes and the sputtering sports car. He began firing and knew he had hit it several times but there was no sign of Jennifer losing control. He continued to fire as Linda pulled alongside, until Jennifer slammed on the brakes, and instead of being the pursuer, he was now the pursued.

The end of the chase came when Linda missed the curve and they flew off the road into the desert. When she was finally able to bring the Mercedes to a stop, Lennie pushed her out of the drivers seat and ordered her to move around to the passenger's side while he took the wheel.

He angrily swung the car around and looked for a way back to the road. By the time he found it, Jennifer and Lorraine had escaped. He suspected they might be in the church parking lot where they had taken refuge, but with the armed choir members milling around, he decided to leave.

Barnes did not tell York and Whittnor about the botched attempt on the women's lives. He didn't have to. They already knew. Upon learning that George Brensley's wife was the target, they suspected he was involved.

It didn't alter their plans for Lennie. Added to the discovery of his increasing use of drugs, his irrational behavior, and the embezzlement that was threatening to bring down the much larger plans his superiors had in mind for Wiley Electronics, both he and his sister would have to be eliminated, sooner rather than later.

Linda was to be killed immediately, but for the time being, Barnes was still useful. "I have one more job for you tonight," York told him as he took him aside, away from Linda, and explained what had to be done. "Somebody's been doing some talking about our business, and all reports are, it's your sister. I want you to take care of it now before she does any more talking. You know what I mean!?"

Lennie knew what it meant. He had heard the same orders on other occasions when he was instructed to get rid of someone. He was going to have to kill his own sister.

"Couldn't someone else do it?"

"No. I want you to do it," York said,

showing his own contempt for Lennie. Just as Barnes enjoyed using the people who worked for him on the streets to push drugs, York enjoyed using him.

York didn't tell him the method that was to be used, and Lennie had his own ideas on how to embarrass his superiors. At the same time, he could show his contempt and hatred for George Brensley and Jim Wiley.

He and Linda drove to Wiley Electronics where he removed any evidence he could find that could link himself to the embezzlement, and then he shot her. But he missed the note that Linda had written to describe where computers could be found and some invoices from Sandstorm Distribution that she had placed behind other paperwork by mistake.

Before he could look further, he was warned by the security guard that Jim Wiley was coming, and that a cop and others were with him. He hurriedly wrapped up his search for incrimination documents and escaped with Lindsay on his heels.

York and Whittnor were livid when they discovered where he had shot his sister and left her for dead, but he didn't care. He hated them almost as much as he hated Wiley and Brensley. In his distorted mind, he was waiting for the day when he could eliminate Whittnor, take over his position in the organization, and live permanently in the estate he was supposed to own.

Whittnor had other plans. He had one more job for Lennie before he was done away with. They still had to make the exchange of drugs for guns at Wiley Electronics, and he wanted him to drive the Sandstorm truck. He could have had someone else drive it, but he wanted Lennie. It was his way of letting Barnes know just how unimportant he really was. When the operation was complete, he would be disposed of.

Lennie did not like the idea of exchanging the drugs at that time. He wanted to lie low for a few days until everything cooled down. He especially did not want to make the exchange at Wiley Electronics. He didn't know how much Wiley and Brensley had discovered or how much they had told the police, but he was sure they would be on their guard.

"Why not make the exchange at the junkyard?" he suggested.

"Because it's being watched," he was told.

"What about Whittnor Trucking?"

"It's also being watched," Whittnor said.

Whittnor was suspicious that his trucking company was being watched, but even if it wasn't, he did not want the exchange to be made there. If there was going to be any trouble, he wanted his company and himself to be as far removed as possible.

Barnes, Salder, and Ellis arrived at Wiley Electronics' shipping department at the same time the tractor trailer from Mexico arrived.

The Sandstorm truck contained several containers of guns and ammunition that were to be moved to the concealed compartment in the Whittnor trailer that was already parked in the warehouse, waiting for the next time it would be scheduled to go across the border.

Then drugs would be transferred from the tractor trailer that had just arrived, to the Sandstorm truck. They would be hidden in a warehouse until another driver arrived to transport them to other destinations around the country. Whittnor and York would never tell him what the destinations were, but he was certain they included cities in the east.

When Lennie arrived, he followed the tractor trailer through the doorway and parked between it and the Whittnor trailer. They had transferred the guns and ammunition and had finished moving the shipment of drugs to the Sandstorm truck when he decided to kill Ellis and Salder. The lure of the briefcase full of money that was to be traded for the drugs, and the drugs themselves, were enough to make him risk his life and go for everything. Salder and

Ellis were foolish enough to trust him, and to make sure they wouldn't be alive to talk, he shot them both.

He was expecting trouble, and when Lindsay barked out his orders from the darkness, to freeze, he ran for the Sandstorm truck. He made an attempt to grab the briefcase containing the money for drugs, but quickly changed his mind when a bullet went through the mirror on the door beside his head. When the tractor trailer rammed through the shipping door, he drove the Sandstorm truck through the splintered hole that it left behind.

At the main gate, the security guard, who had been doing his job by pretending to read the centerfold in his magazine and ignore what was taking place, heard the gunfire. When the tractor trailer burst through the shipping door, he quickly decided to run for his life. His decision saved his life, temporarily. For once, he hoped the police would pick him up, before Lennie found him.

Barnes did not take the same route as the tractor trailer. He didn't know where it was going, Whittnor had looked after that part, and he didn't care. He was too busy trying to save his own skin. He headed in the other direction and hid the Sandstorm truck in the warehouse where he had been instructed to take it.

"Where the hell are they?" York demanded when told about the narrow escape from the shipping department and having to leave the weapons and cash behind.

"How should I know," Lennie replied. "You're the one who said we should make the exchange at Wiley Electronics."

Barnes enjoyed throwing the problem back at his boss. It was one of the few times he was able to get some revenge for the way York treated him. It would be nice to see him get into trouble with his superiors for a change.

The next day, when he heard that Salder and Ellis were confirmed dead, he had only one thought. Now he was going to have to find someone else to push his drugs and take the fall for him.

His superiors had other ideas for Lennie Barnes.

SEVENTEEN

Joanne Kent, Wiley Electronics International Sales Manager, had flown in from Europe to set up the presentation of computers and other equipment that was to take place at their New York sales office the following day.

She greeted Jim when he arrived and briefed him on what he could expect from Louise Fisher, a purchasing representative for some of their more important buyers.

"Louise insisted you be present," she said. "And I wasn't about to argue. This meeting is much too important for the company."

She smiled. "You do know the real reason why Louise wants you here, don't you."

Jim knew. The personality clash that existed between the two women was not obvious, but it sometimes smoldered a little beneath the surface. So he decided it was just as well he had returned for the meeting. Several million dollars in computers and parts sales hinged on the outcome.

He occasionally drew mental comparisons of Louise and Joanne in an effort to determine why they had difficulty getting along. They were both beautiful business women who were strong willed, knew what they wanted, were not afraid to go after it, and almost always were able to get it.

Perhaps, he thought, that was why they did not see eye to eye. They had too many things in common that they both wanted, with him sometimes rising to the top of their, what he liked to call, things to do list.

He really never knew how high he was on their lists, exactly when he landed there, or how serious they were on any particular day, because their business careers always came first. Even so, he could feel an air of sensuality when either, or both of them, were near. Maybe the difference was that Joanne had accepted that he was not prepared for a long term relationship and she would have to wait, while Louise hadn't.

Still, there was a mutual, if sometimes begrudging respect between the two women. "Louise is a great sales representative," Joanne had told Jim, "but she's not for you. You would have to count your socks every morning to make sure she hadn't sold them to one of her buyers."

Jim did not want to get involved with an in-company romance. But at the same time, he thought of Jennifer Brookbaine and how mixing pleasure with business in Westland seemed alright. It was ironic that Louise would pursue him with invitations to spend the night, while Jennifer, a woman he couldn't help but think about spending the rest of his life with, would leave him at her door with a goodnight kiss.

In his office, he called a flower shop and had a dozen roses sent to Jennifer with a card thanking her for her help in the investigation in Westland. Then he telephoned to ask if she had discovered anything new, which was as much to hear her voice as it was an inquiry.

Jim found himself wanting to tell her he was falling in love with her, but stopped. He couldn't possibly be, not in such a short time, and he didn't know for sure how she felt about him.

"Besides," he grumbled to himself as he hung up the phone. "I shouldn't be mixing business and pleasure."

He knew the sales presentation would be interesting. He joked with Joanne about her relationship with Louise Fisher and asked if she was prepared for the meeting. She said she would wisely stay out of the way at the other end of the room while Jim was seduced by Louise's charms.

Louise was as beautiful as ever. Like Joanne, she was dressed in business attire that showed her authority without hiding her femininity.

"It's so nice to see you" she said, taking his hand in both of hers and squeezing. Then she hugged him and pressed a cheek against his.

The hug was always welcome. "Nice to see you too, Louise," he responded warmly. "How are you?"

"Just fine. How many of these machines are you going to try to sell me today?"

"As many as I can."

"Which is your best one?"

Jim pointed to a computer that had recently been introduced into the market. "That one over there."

"And the worst?"

"You know we don't have a worst." He showed her another computer that didn't look much different from the first one. "That one has less features, but it still does a very good job."

He did not tell Louise that it was also much less expensive than the first computer. He didn't have to. She would already know. She would also put both computers through every test she had learned in her years of sales. In the end, she would make her decision based on what each was worth and what the companies she represented needed.

When she finished testing each computer's features and had asked her last question, she opened her briefcase and removed some forms. She laid them neatly on a table and entered figures based on each system's list price, less discounts she expected with the quantities she was ordering.

"Acceptable?" she asked.

Jim inspected the figures she had written on the forms. "Acceptable," he replied. Like Louise, he had known before they arrived at the meeting, approximately what the quantities would be and what she would be prepared to pay.

"Good," she said. "I'll have a purchase order issued as soon as I return to my office."

As they left the meeting room, she took his hand in hers again. "What are you doing this evening?"

"I'm afraid I have to return to Westland for a few days," he said, trying to make it sound urgent.

"What are you doing right now?"

"Right now I have to go down to the warehouse to check on some shipping schedules."

She squeezed his hand a little tighter. "Can I come with you?"

"Sure, come on along," he replied. "I'm just going to be a few minutes."

As they walked, Louise asked why he had to

return to Westland so soon. He told her about the embezzlement by Lennie Barnes, the shootout in the shipping department, and the mysterious truck from Sandstorm Distribution for which they weren't able to find a street address.

"I think you might see something in your shipping department here that will be of interest to you," she said. "If the driver hasn't already taken care of business and left."

Instead of going to Jim's office, they turned and walked toward the shipping area. Louise pointed to a transport truck that was just pulling away from the dock.

On its side, Sandstorm Distribution was painted.

"Look familiar?" she said. "I saw it driving in when I arrived. It appears that your Sandstorm Distribution isn't as mysterious as you thought it was."

Alan Jamison, their shipping supervisor, met them in the shipping office. "We started doing business with Sandstorm a few weeks ago," he said. "It's a small freight company right here in New York. They usually don't deal in large shipments. That's probably why you haven't seen them before. They combine smaller orders from different suppliers and then transport them to other parts of the country."

"That come from Westland?"

"Yes."

"Do you know if they prepare orders for export?"

"Sometimes."

"To Mexico, Europe, other countries?"

"I think so. We don't always know the final destinations."

"Do you know who hired them?"

"Joanne Kent. She said they came in and offered her a good deal, so she accepted it. So far we haven't had any problems."

"Do you know where they're located, in case I want to get some more information on them?"

Jamison looked up the address of Sandstorm Distribution and gave it to him. "Is there some difficulty I should know about?" he asked.

"No, I just hadn't seen them in here before and wondered who they were," Jim answered, deciding there would be time later to fill him in, after he talked to Joanne Kent about her decision to hire Sandstorm.

Jim's mind was racing as they walked out of the shipping office. Now he knew why they couldn't find an address, other than a mail box, for Sandstorm Distribution in Westland. Because it wasn't in Westland. It was in New York. There had to be a connection somehow between Sandstorm Distribution, the drugs for weapons trade, his New York office, and possibly even their international facilities. He didn't know what the connection was, but he was determined to find out.

He grabbed Louise by the shoulders and held her in front of him. "Louise, you are the greatest purchasing agent in the world." And then he hugged her tightly.

Other employees stared at them. It was a show of enthusiastic affection they did not see often from Jim Wiley. It was also a show of affection that Louise Fisher was not expecting, but she made the best of it. She hugged him back.

When they broke apart she leaned against his arms to catch her breath. "You could be setting a dangerous precedent," she said as she glanced sideways at the people watching them.

Jim was catching his own breath. "I might not be able to take you out this evening, but you would be the most appreciated lunch date a man ever had."

"On one condition," she said.

"Anything," he promised.

"You tell me everything that is going on with you and Sandstorm Distribution."

Jim happily agreed. As they ate lunch, he filled her in on the rest of the story, from when John Wilson had called, informing him of the embezzlement in Westland, up to where Louise told him of seeing the Sandstorm truck entering the shipping department in New York.

"Now you know why you're appreciated so much," he said. "You have just given me the connection that might help us tie this whole thing together."

"What are you going to do now?" she asked.

Wiley set his lower jaw and looked at her across the table. "I'm going to visit Sandstorm Distribution and see if I can discover what the hell they're doing."

EIGHTEEN

Sandstorm Distribution's warehouse was an hour's drive from Wiley Electronics New York office. Jim Wiley was not alone. Louise Fisher had insisted he take her with him.

"If nothing else," she said, "you owe me for giving you the Sandstorm connection."

Jim emphasized to her once again how vicious the Sandstorm people could be, and that if the people in New York belonged to the same crime family he had encountered in Westland, their lives could be in danger.

She insisted anyway. "You are not going without me," she stated flatly. "And that's that. Besides, I might be able to help you."

As they made their way through the busy New York traffic, Louise asked him to go over once again all the information they had shared at lunch. She was particularly interested when Jim discussed the hours he had spent alone with Jennifer Brookbaine. Seeing a change in his expression, she pumped him with more questions about the time he had been with her as they tracked down Lennie Barnes.

"This Jennifer," she inquired, "is she beautiful?"

"Yes," Jim said. "She is beautiful. In many ways she's like you."

"Do you like her?" Louise pressed.

"Yes, I like her."

"A lot?"

Jim began to squirm. He remembered Louise's knack of knowing when someone was attempting to avoid a question.

"I just met her," he said.

"Do you like me?"

"Of course I like you."

"As much as you like this Jennifer Brookbaine?"

Jim was quiet.

"Well?"

"It's not quite the same," he said. "You are a beautiful successful independent business woman who can have any man she wants, and Jennifer is . . ."

Louise finished his sentence. "A beautiful successful independent business woman who can have any man she wants."

"I suppose," he said.

"So, what's the difference?"

"I don't know," he replied. "I consider myself lucky to know each of you. There is just a difference."

"I think I know what the difference is," she said.

"What?"

"You're in love with Jennifer."

Jim was quiet again. The more he thought about Jennifer, the more he was beginning to believe he was falling in love with her.

"We're almost at Sandstorm Distribution," he said, changing the subject.

They found a parking space and walked a short distance until they stood across the street from the Sandstorm warehouse. It was not an impressive building. The old wooden siding was run down, gray and dirty, and a window that looked out onto the street was protected by iron bars and painted over so no one could see in. A door with a much smaller bar covered painted window stood at what appeared to be the entrance to the office.

Ten feet away was a shipping door high enough to accommodate vehicles such as the Sandstorm truck. It was closed, with no windows to see inside.

Louise didn't wait for Jim to make the first move. "Come on," she said, pulling him by the arm.

They crossed the street and stood in front of the building at the entrance to the office. Louise grabbed the aging door handle, put her thumb on the latch, and pushed. When the door didn't open, she knocked. When there was no response from inside, she knocked again as hard as she could.

"It doesn't look like anybody's home," Jim said when there was still no answer. He looked around for another entrance. "So it might be a good time to visit. I think I'll see if there's another way in."

Louise followed him to an alley at the side of the building where he once again tried to emphasize how dangerous the people involved with Sandstorm Distribution could be. "Do you know what could happen to us if they find us in there?" he said.

"Yes," she replied. "They'll probably throw us out on our ear. I don't think they're going to call the cops."

"Their biggest problem will probably be deciding where to bury our bodies after they shoot us," he said. "I wish you would wait out here and let me have a look inside, and then we can call the police."

"No," she exclaimed, grabbing his arm and pulling him along the side of the building. "You're going to have to take me with you, because you are not going alone."

Jim didn't offer more protest. "Let's try this," he said, stopping at a doorway part way down an alley.

Louise put her ear to the door and listened

for movement inside. "Do you think we can break it down?" she asked.

Jim put his shoulder against the door and pushed. It didn't budge. He hit it with his shoulder. There was still no movement. "Not unless I suddenly turn into Superman," he quipped as he peered through another iron bar covered, painted pane of glass.

"How about this?" Louise said as he looked around the alley for something he could use to break the window.

Jim looked at the spiked heel shoe he was offered, then at the door. He looked at the shoe one more time before handing it back to her. Finally, he picked up a piece of broken concrete and drove a corner of it through the window. With a noise that seemed to fill the alley, the pane shattered into the building.

They glanced around and listened for sounds of someone approaching. When they were sure they had not been discovered, Jim reached through the bars and found a latch on the inside of the door. He pulled it back and pushed. The door creaked as it swung inward. It would not open all the way because of wooden crates that had been stacked in front of it, but it moved enough so that they were able to squeeze through.

They made their way between the piles of

supplies. In light that filtered down through windows in the roof, they could make out the shipping area and materials that were used to prepare crates and cartons for shipment.

A Sandstorm Distribution truck was backed into the dock. They could not tell if it was the same one that had been at Wiley Electronics New York shipping department, although from the markings on cartons that had been unloaded, they guessed it was.

"What should I look for?" Louise asked as she watched Jim move to a packing bench and examine cartons that had been prepared for delivery.

"Anything that looks suspicious," he said, "especially anything going to or coming from Wiley Electronics."

"Would cases of automatic weapons and boxes of ammunition qualify?" Louise asked, lifting up the top of a container. "They don't have address labels, but I suppose they probably wouldn't stop long enough in your company to need them. It looks like Sandstorm Distribution is picking up drugs in Westland for transportation to New York, and at the same time delivering guns and ammunition to Westland for shipment to Mexico."

"And I think I might have found how they transport the drugs," Jim said. "This pallet of computers was enclosed with a plastic wrap before it was shipped from Westland, for protection. The plastic has been torn open and cartons have been removed. Also, the cartons are sealed at the factory and aren't supposed to be opened until they reach their destination. These cartons have been opened, tampered with, and then taped shut again."

Two cartons were sitting on a bench near the pallet. Their markings and shipping address labels showed they were manufactured in Westland by Wiley Electronics. Jim slit the tape on a carton, opened it, and lifted out the computer. It appeared normal.

He put the computer aside and continued to search. At the end of the table was another computer. It was the same as the one he had just inspected, except it had been taken out of the carton and had its covers removed.

On the outside of the computer, everything was normal. Keypads, switches, fuse holders, line cord receptacles, anything that was visible was still present.

Inside, components were missing. Printed circuit boards, power supplies, cooling fans, and everything else including the brackets that once held parts in position, had been removed.

In their place, wrapped in plastic bags and tape similar to the kind he had seen Lennie

Barnes and his friends moving from the tractor trailer that had arrived at Wiley Electronics to the Sandstorm truck, was the same type of package.

"Did you find what you're looking for?"

Jim stopped, then slowly turned to look at the barrel of the gun that was pointed at him.

The man that was holding it was large, and his driver's uniform threatened to split as it stretched over his massive frame. A thin black tie hung from his neck. It didn't do its job, which was to cover the buttons on the bulging openings at the front of his shirt.

His voice matched his appearance. "Did you find what you're looking for?" he demanded again.

"Not everything," Jim answered.

"We're looking for the owner or whoever runs this place," Louise broke in. "We do business with your company, and we want to talk to them."

The man looked at her suspiciously. "How did you get in here?"

"The door was open," Louise stammered. "We just came in to . . ."

"The door was locked," he snapped. "Now, how did you get in here?"

"The door was open," she repeated. "We closed it when we came . . ."

He pointed the gun at her and squeezed his finger against the trigger. "One more time, how did you get in here?"

"Through the back," Jim said. "We came in through a side door."

"How?"

"We broke a window." There didn't seem to be any sense lying to him. He was going to find out anyway.

"Get over there," he said, motioning with the gun for Louise to stand beside Jim. With the weapon still pointed at them, he walked to a desk at the other side of the room and picked up a telephone.

"How fast can you get between those crates and out the door we came in through?" Jim whispered to Louise.

"Faster than you can," she answered. "I don't think he's calling his mother."

They turned together and ran. The crack of the gun going off echoed through the building as bullets crashing into pallets of goods behind them. Jim grabbed at anything he could pull into the narrow passageway to block the path between them and the gunman, until they reached the doorway and pushed their way through into the alley. With one last burst of fear and energy, they ran toward the street and safety.

Behind them, they could hear the man as he clawed at the door, trying to open it wide enough for his massive body to pass through. Fortunately, his heavy frame prevented an easy exit and it gave them the time they needed to escape.

As they sped away, Louise watched the road behind for signs that they were being followed. When she was sure no one was in pursuit, she wrapped her hands around Jim's arm and relaxed beside him. "I didn't know life with you could be so exciting," she said.

"Believe me, I'd be quite happy if it wasn't," he replied. "I thought that all my excitement had ended with the gunfight at Wiley Electronics in Westland, but it looks like we're on the trail of something else."

She moved closer to him. "We?"

"Me," he said, correcting himself. "You've done enough. I really do appreciate your help, but I don't want to get you involved in any more danger."

"All right," she said, "but promise me you'll call if there's anything I can do to help."

"I promise," he replied.

"Remember," she said as she opened the door of his car at Wiley Electronics and prepared to climb out, "you promised to call me if you need help."

Then she leaned across the seat and kissed him on the lips.

As she climbed into her own car and drove out of the parking lot, Jim thought once again about the similarities between Louise Fisher and Jennifer.

NINETEEN

After midnight, Westland Airport was not busy. As with his last visit, Jim had arranged with George Brensley to meet him. He looked around the arrivals area, expecting to see him.

"Jim."

Jennifer was there. She was a welcome sight as she walked toward him. She took his hands in hers the same way Louise Fisher had a few hours earlier, except this time the feeling was different. She looked at him for a moment, then let his hands go and threw her arms around his neck.

She hugged him tightly and kissed him. "I'm glad you're back," she said when she finally let go. "I've missed you."

Jim broke into a happy smile. "Me too. This is a lot more fun than hugging George."

He looked around. "Where is George?"

"Oh, he had a meeting or something to go to with Lorraine."

"At this hour?"

"That's what I said. At this hour?"

"What did Lorraine say?"

"Shut up and get to the airport. I have a

feeling their meeting was in their bedroom watching a late show on T.V. or whatever else they do there."

"I'll have to thank Lorraine, and George," Jim said. "I have some news that I think will help us piece this whole guns for drugs thing together."

"I have some news for you too," Jennifer answered, "but let's hear your news first."

They exchanged information on the way out of the terminal. Jim told her about Louise Fisher pointing out the Sandstorm Distribution truck at Wiley Electronics shipping department in New York.

"Louise Fisher? Where have I heard that name?"

Jim could feel Jennifer's eyes looking more deeply into his. The same intuition that Louise had when someone wanted to avoid a question was there.

"She's a purchasing representative who buys computers and digital systems from Wiley Electronics for other companies. She went with me to the Sandstorm Distribution warehouse, where we broke in and almost got shot."

"Oh."

"We couldn't find a street address for Sandstorm in Westland because it isn't in Westland. It's in New York."

"How did they come to be doing business with your company?"

"A good price. Our shipping supervisor said they gave Joanne Kent a good deal and she hired them. I talked to Joanne. She said they had been in business a long time and appeared reputable. I thought I would have you look into their past history to see who owns them."

"I'll get on it, first thing in the morning. So they're using Whittnor Transportation trucks to bring drugs in from Mexico, switching them to the Sandstorm trucks at Wiley Electronics, and then taking them to New York to be put into emptied computer housings for shipment elsewhere."

"That's it. Then weapons and ammunition are coming this way in the same Sandstorm trucks, to be exchanged at Wiley Electronics for shipment to Mexico."

"Was there room in the computer housings for many drugs?"

"Lots of room. It was just a matter of leaving the outsides intact, ripping out the insides, and filling them with whatever drugs they wanted shipped. Then they put them back together and sealed up the cartons until they reached their destination. We think most of it was done in New York, but they probably also did some at the junkyard here, and other places."

"Where would shipments go from New York? Other cities on the east coast?"

"Probably, and other countries. We saw some delivery labels with international addresses. Who would think of looking inside a computer for drugs?"

"You would," Jennifer said. "But they seemed to go to a lot of trouble to get the drugs from Mexico to New York. When they got across the border, why didn't they just head east?"

"Probably because a truck carrying products from Mexico would look more suspicious, the farther east it went. With all the inspection stations on the highways, they would be afraid they might be checked more thoroughly and the drugs discovered."

"So they paid off the security guard at Wiley Electronics to act as a lookout, or look the other way, and switched the drugs to the Sandstorm truck in your shipping department. But why your company?"

"I don't know. And we can't ask the security guard, yet. But we will, just as soon as Lieutenant Lindsay tracks him down. The way Barnes has been killing everyone around him, he'll talk, if for no other reason than to save his own skin. And I'm sure the Lieutenant will convince him to identify any other men who were at the shipping department for the exchange, and who they work for."

Jennifer nodded in agreement. "As far as we know, they're all employed by Whittnor Transportation. The Whittnor trailer is still sitting at your shipping dock, with the hidden compartment empty and waiting for someone to come and get it. The police have undercover officers keeping an eye on it."

"Maybe they'll forget about it and leave it there."

"I'm not so sure. Neither is Lieutenant Lindsay. He hopes their curiosity and greed will eventually get the best of them and they'll come after it. If they think the weapons are still there, they'd be worth a lot of money to somebody, not to mention Whittnor and York and Barnes' necks when they don't deliver."

"What company do you think they'll use to exchange the drugs for weapons, now that their outlet at Wiley Electronics shipping department has been discovered?"

"Maybe the junkyard. They might still believe it's in the clear. When Lieutenant Lindsay learned his stakeout had been discovered, he pulled it off and put another one on that was a little less conspicuous. He has someone sitting in the attic of a building across the street."

"How does the junkyard fit into all this?"

"We believe it's being used for small deals, up to a hundred thousand dollars or so."

"Small deals?"

"That's small in the drug world. What they took to New York would be measured in millions."

"Have the police discovered anyone else involved, other than Barnes and his friends?"

"Some smaller dealers they've suspected of selling for a long time, but have never been able to pin anything on. They followed a couple of them from the junkyard and picked them up with the drugs hidden in their car. Apparently they're talking up a storm, trying to save their own necks. Lieutenant Lindsay says they're keeping them on ice until they see how many more they can catch."

"Won't they be missed?"

"Eventually, but he hopes not until the police can do some real damage to their operation."

"What about Lennie?"

"They saw him at the junkyard, but haven't seen him since. Lindsay wonders if his past transgressions against the mob have finally caught up to him. Lorraine will be disappointed. She wanted to hang him."

"So who do you think is the big boss? We know it can't be Lennie Barnes, and probably not Charlie York. What about the owner of the trucking company, Jerry Whittnor?"

"I don't think so, and neither does the Westland Police Department. They might look big here but they're small potatoes if you look at the entire picture. Lindsay suspects someone in New York, perhaps whoever owns Sandstorm Distribution."

"Could be. Sandstorm ships to companies all over the world. That could also be why they picked our company. They knew our shipping procedures, they figured no one would suspect they were using it, and we also ship all over the world. They also knew which security guard could be bought and which past employees could be used."

"And which employee in your company is still being used. They still have someone on the inside. Charlie York said that Lennie was supposed to contact someone in the shipping department."

"Any suspects?"

"Not suspects, but Carl Rogers, John Wilson, and Paul Cater were at the Mayor's Charity Ball tonight at the estate, and Jerry Whittnor spent quite a bit of time talking to them. He could be using them without their knowing. Of course, there were a lot of other people at the gala, prominent people, and Whittnor was chummy with most of them, so talking to your employees probably doesn't mean anything."

"I agree," Jim said. "But all the same, I'll ask them what Whittnor wanted to talk about. Unless you want me to wait."

"Could you wait a day or so?" Jennifer asked. "Lindsay believes that whatever is happening is going to happen soon, and he doesn't want to tip anyone off."

"Anything else that was interesting?"

"Yes. There is something else going on at that estate. Whittnor and York spent a lot of time standing in front of one of the rooms, with a couple goon like characters at the door. They all appeared to be fidgeting, like they were nervous and waiting for someone."

"Maybe expecting their bosses?"

"Could be. Whittnor had someone from the east coast picked up at the airport earlier tonight. It was a private jet, away from the terminal. No one saw who it was."

"I think I'd be nervous too, if I had to explain Lennie Barnes, the missing money, and guns they think are waiting in a truck in our shipping department that they can't get to, and aren't there anyway."

"I know. The room was the one place they didn't want anyone near. Lorraine and I did anyway, and we were quickly escorted away."

"Lorraine was there with you?"

"Yes. Harry Haddel was supposed to be my date, but he couldn't make it. Lorraine and I were Mr. and Mrs. A. Smythe. Lorraine got the tickets at her office. Apparently the Smythes were out of town and couldn't attend. I was Al and she was Alexis, or she was Al and I was Alexis, I forget. Anyway, we told the guards at the gate that we were friends of Whittnor and they let us in."

"Wasn't that dangerous?"

"A little. When we were ordered out of the house, a couple of the goons followed us and tried to stop us from leaving, until Lieutenant Lindsay came to our rescue."

"Lindsay?"

"Lindsay, official uniform and all. He escorted us out to my car, like he actually liked us, and stood in front of the goons' car until we were out of sight."

"What are the police going to do about Whittnor and York?"

"For the present, leave them where they are, and see if they lead them to whoever is really in charge."

Jim smiled his approval. "So it appears that Wiley Electronics is still going to require your services as a private investigator."

"I was hoping you would say that," Jennifer

answered. "And it will give me an excuse to spend some more time with you. How about my place for a late night snack, so we can discuss it some more?"

"My pleasure. But what about Sheeba? I have a feeling she's not too crazy about me."

"She likes you. She's just a little jealous, that's all. And if she isn't nice, I'll have a talk with her."

"What are we having?"

"Something light. I was hoping you would say yes, so I put something out on the counter to thaw while I came to pick you up. You can relax while I prepare it. I shouldn't take too long . . . unless Sheeba has eaten it."

Sheeba's nose had let her down. The food was still there. While Jennifer prepared their snack, Jim relaxed on the sofa. When she looked in a few minutes later, he was fast asleep with Sheeba curled up on the floor beside him.

Without waking him she covered him with a blanket.

"Oh well," she said to Sheeba, "maybe we can have dinner tomorrow night."

TWENTY

Jim was still sleeping when Jennifer awoke early the following morning. She gazed at him as he slept and then at her dog that had decided they could be friends after all.

She found a note pad to scratch a few lines to explain where she was going. "Didn't want to wake you," she wrote. "Have gone to Lennie Barnes' estate to look for evidence. Be back in a couple hours. Love Jennifer."

She quietly slipped out of the house, leaving the man she was falling in love with and her dog asleep on the sofa. She had considered waking him and then changed her mind, deciding that he needed a rest after his late night flight from the east coast.

She drove to the estate that Lennie Barnes supposedly owned and where the Mayor's Charitable Ball was held. The property appeared even larger than it had the night before. She passed by several times, searching for a way to get in, then parked across the street to consider her options.

As she watched, a pickup truck pulling landscaping equipment on a trailer stopped at the gate. An arm reached from an open window, a security code was entered, and the iron gate swung open.

Without hesitating, Jennifer turned around and followed the truck through. It wasn't until she was inside that she wondered about what she had done, whether the crew in the truck had noticed her following, and if they had, would they ignore her, thinking she was another guest, or would they report her? Deciding they probably wouldn't care one way or the other, she continued to follow.

At the first opportunity, she pulled off the driveway behind some shrubbery and looked around to make sure she hadn't been discovered. Unless the landscapers had reported her, there was enough foliage between where she stopped and the house to prevent anyone who happened to look out from seeing her.

She made her way to the rear of the building, crossed a patio to what appeared to be an entrance to the kitchen area, and peered in through a window. Deciding that knocking would be a good way to discover if anyone was home, but a worse way to be escorted off the property, she took a quick look over her shoulder, another look through the window, then tried the door. It was unlocked.

She stepped inside and silently made her way across the kitchen to a hallway that led to the rest of the house. On the other side of the hallway was the locked door to the room that had been guarded so closely the night before during the ball.

Manipulating the set of lock-picks that Harry Haddel had given her and taught her how to use, she opened the door and began looking for evidence that could link Jerry Whittnor and Charlie York to the guns for drugs exchange at Wiley Electronics.

She searched unlocked drawers in the only desk in the room for references to Sandstorm Distribution or Wiley Electronics. Finding none, she moved to the file cabinets along a wall, opening one and then another. She stopped when she heard a door close somewhere in the house.

At the opposite end of the room were two doors. A strip of light streamed out from under one of them. The other was in darkness. Choosing the second door, she turned off the main overhead light in the room, opened one half of a sliding partition, and slipped inside a closet.

Her hand reached into her purse and clutched her thirty-eight revolver, then she stood quietly and stared through the small opening between the two parts of the door, waiting for whoever had entered the house.

In the dim light, she could make out the forms of three people entering the room. They were arguing.

"I tell you, we have to get the trailer out of Wiley Electronics now," she heard one of them say. "If we don't move it from the shipping area, it's just a matter of time until they find the hidden compartment." The voice belonged to Charlie York.

"We can't move it," the other man replied. This voice belonged to Jerry Whittnor. "They're onto us, and if we try to move it right now, they'll get it, and us. If Barnes got rid of Wiley and Brensley at the airport the way he was supposed to, we wouldn't be having these problems, and if he hadn't been embezzling money, we'd still be using Wiley Electronics' shipping department and no one would be any the wiser."

The third person spoke for the first time. It was a woman's voice that Jennifer thought she recognized. "Forget what we should have done," she said. "The important thing is to get the Sandstorm truck into the junkyard and onto the road with the shipment. By the time it gets to the east coast we'll have an alternate place to drop it. We can't use the Sandstorm warehouse in New York anymore because they know where it is now and how we used it."

"What about Wiley and Brensley and that private investigator they hired?"

"Forget them. They can't hurt us since we'll no longer be using Sandstorm, and we won't be using Wiley Electronics shipping department again so they'll be satisfied in knowing they stopped their leak."

"What about the stakeout at the junkyard?"

"I've been informed that the stakeout is gone," she said. "Besides, the junkyard is the only place we have left to make the switch. Every other place is being watched."

"When are we getting the guns at Wiley Electronics?"

"Forget the guns. We'll order another shipment, and take the loss. Besides, we don't even know if they are still in the shipping department. I'll have to explain the delay, but it's better than ending up in jail with everyone else that the police have nabbed. And I've been watching the truck in the shipping department. There are a couple people hanging around that I don't recognize, and I think they could be with the police."

"Where are we getting the money for the new shipment of guns?" York asked.

"It's in the safe," the woman answered.

Jennifer could see the woman's outline as she crossed the room to where a bookcase was located. She swung a section of it aside to reveal a safe that was hidden in the wall. In a moment she opened the safe, reached inside, closed it and the section, turned back to the men, and handed Whittnor a bundle of bills. They talked for a few more minutes and then left the room.

Questions raced through Jennifer's mind. Who was the woman whose voice she thought she recognized, and what was her role in all this? And why would she have the combination to a safe in Lennie Barnes' home? Unless she owned it.

When she was sure there were no sounds, she moved to where the safe was hidden in the bookcase. The woman had not closed it all the way and she was able to open the door and look inside.

She pulled out the contents and examined them, stopping at a folder with a Sandstorm Distribution label. Inside were papers and bills of lading indicating trips that had been taken between Wiley Electronics in Westland and cities on the east coast.

She stuffed the papers into her handbag, moved across the room to the hallway, passed into the kitchen area, and left through the rear doorway that led outside to the patio.

When she turned the corner of the building, she stopped. A few feet away were Jerry

Whittnor and Charlie York. The men each had a gun pointed in her direction. With them was the woman whose voice Jennifer thought she recognized.

"What do we have here?" the woman asked.

"She's the private investigator that Wiley hired," Whittnor said.

The woman's eyes opened a little wider. "I know who she is. Nice to see you again, Ms. Brookbaine?"

At about the same time, a telephone was ringing beside the sleeping Jim Wiley. He rolled over and picked it up.

"Jennifer Brookbaine?" The voice on the phone asked.

Jim looked around and saw the note that Jennifer had written. "She isn't here right now. Can I take a message for her?"

"Yes," the caller answered. "I'm a police officer calling from New York. I'm a friend of Harry Haddel. Jennifer asked if I could help her get some information on a shipping company here, Sandstorm Distribution. She said that someone made a call from Sandstorm yesterday afternoon, and she wanted to know who the call was to."

"We traced the call to Wiley Electronics in Westland," he continued, "to a person in the manufacturing department."

Jim listened again, recognizing the telephone call as the one the man in the Sandstorm warehouse was making when he and Louise Fisher were running for their lives.

The call was to his head electronics technician and quality control supervisor that Jennifer had been introduced to during her first visit to Wiley Electronics.

Angelina Bales.

TWENTY-ONE

The same high fence and security gate that Jennifer had faced earlier met Jim Wiley and George Brensley when they arrived at the Barnes Estate to search for her.

As they discussed the best way to get through the gate, it swung open and a gray Mercedes limo swept out of the driveway and onto the street. Like the other limos they had seen, the licence plate was familiar. They could not make out who was in the car because of the tinted windows. The gate swung shut again before any thought could be given to entering the property that way.

"Move the car alongside the fence," Jim said. "As close as you can get."

"What about the Mercedes?" George asked as he drove off the pavement and onto the grass.

"Follow it," Jim said. "When you find where it's going, call Lorraine. Tell her to pick up Sheeba and to meet us. I'm sure Jennifer is either inside the estate or in that car, and the dog might be able to help us locate her. I'll call you as soon as I see what's going on here."

He scrambled onto a fender of the car, then the roof, reached for a tree branch, swung himself over, and dropped to the ground inside. As George sped away after the Mercedes, he looked around to make sure he hadn't been detected. Ahead, he could see Jennifer's vehicle, hidden in the foliage.

As Jennifer had done earlier, he walked to the rear of the house where the door to the kitchen was still unlocked. With no sounds of activity inside, he moved from room to room, searching for any indication that she had been there. Finding none, he left through the same doorway he had entered and searched the surrounding area.

The reflection of a set of keys on the patio caught his eye. They were the same set Jennifer had used the night before, complete with a border collie etched into a silver charm and keys to her car. With a new feeling of urgency, he called Lorraine.

"George just phoned again," she informed him. "He followed the Mercedes to the junkyard where you and he used to play. He said you would know where to meet him, on the side street. I'll be there too, with Sheeba." Before he could tell her to be careful, she had disconnected.

He ran across the lawn to where Jennifer had hidden her car, used her key to start it, backed onto the driveway, and raced toward the gate.

As the steel bars loomed ahead, he pressed his foot on the accelerator and slammed into it. The twisted metal in both sections flew open. Without slowing, he kept his foot down and raced toward the junkyard.

George was waiting for him on the side street beside the old gate where Jim and Jennifer had entered earlier. Lorraine and Sheeba were with him.

"Have you seen her?" he asked.

"No," George replied. "The car disappeared into the junkyard and I couldn't see what was going on. I called Lieutenant Lindsay. He said he was on his way."

"We can't wait."

Jim was already pulling the sofa away from the hole in the old wooden gate. He swung a board aside and stepped through. George was behind him, behind George was Lorraine, and at Lorraine's side was Sheeba.

They followed the path between the compressed piles of cars and cautiously made their way to the center of the yard. Ahead, was the building where Jim and Jennifer had discovered Lennie Barnes and Charlie York arguing about the drugs for weapons exchange.

Beside the building, Brutus was standing on guard. Before they could worry about the large dog, Sheeba trotted past and sauntered up to him. He perked an ear and wagged his tail. His body undulated as he welcomed a new friend. The two dogs sniffed hello to each other, then strolled out of sight.

With Brutus out of the way, they were able to creep to the back of the building where two men were arguing.

"What time did you tell the Sandstorm truck to be here?" they heard Jerry Whittnor say.

"It should be here now," Charlie York replied. "They said they were on their way half an hour ago. I'll call them again to make sure they're coming."

"What do you want us to do with her?" they heard Whittnor ask.

Angelina Bales spoke for the first time. "Get rid of her."

"We should have gotten rid of her back at the estate," York said.

"And what were you going to do with her after that?" Angelina replied. "We have places to dispose of her around here. So let's do it."

Through the dirty windows, they could see the blurred forms of people moving toward the doorway at the other side of the building. They cautiously looked around the corner just as Jennifer appeared. Close behind her was Angelina Bales. Her hand held a gun that was shoved into the small of Jennifer's back.

"Stop," Lorraine ordered, pointing her small pistol at Angelina.

Angelina halted. Not moving her gun, she turned her head slightly to look at them.

"If I get it, she gets it too," she said.

They stood frozen, Lorraine waiting for Angelina to make a move, and at the same time hoping she wouldn't.

Sheeba solved the stalemate. As Brutus watched in curious interest, she charged from behind the building and grabbed Angelina by the arm. The force spun her around, the gun flew out of her hand, and she dropped to the ground.

Without thinking about the other drug smugglers in the building, Jim ran to Jennifer to make sure she was alright.

"I'm okay," she said, looking up at him, then at the dog that had saved her life and was licking her face.

"You shouldn't have come here, Jim."

Jim turned at the sound of another female voice behind him.

"Hello Louise," he said. "Do I have to ask what brings you to Westland?"

"I think you already know," Louise Fisher answered, "the same reason you came back, or should I say, the same problem, different reason. How did you find out about me?"

"From a police officer in New York," Jim answered. "After he told me about the telephone call to Angelina from the Sandstorm warehouse, he said there was a second call to Angelina. It was from a phone number I recognized. How did you get involved with smuggling drugs and guns? And why?"

"I sort of fell into it," Louise said. "My husband was into drug smuggling for years. I didn't know about it, but he was. He owned Sandstorm Distribution in New York and used it to move drugs around the east coast. When his bosses decided to go international, they began using your company as a connection. Wiley Electronics owned locations they could use, and your computers were an easy way to transport them."

"How did you get into the business?"

"My husband died. Actually, he was murdered. It's a dangerous occupation. Isn't that what you told me in New York? After his death, I went to the Sandstorm warehouse to go over the books and see what kind of business I had inherited. That's when I discovered what he was really into, and how profitable it could be."

"You didn't have to take it over."

"I suppose not. I guess I could have closed Sandstorm Distribution, or turned what I knew over to the police."

"You could have run the business legitimately."

"No, I couldn't. The drugs were the business. Without them, there was no Sandstorm Distribution. Except for companies like Wiley Electronics and a few others that we used to move products around the country, we didn't have any clients."

"You still didn't have to take it over."

"Yes I did. I have bosses too, you know. If I didn't take it over, they would have given it to someone else, and I would have had nothing. If they let me live."

"Nothing would have been better than what you were doing."

"Maybe, except I liked the money. I got used to having a lot of money when my husband ran the operation. I could have said no, but I didn't."

"How did Angelina get involved?"

"Angelina is my sister-in-law. We used to talk a lot, and one day her brother's business deals came up in the conversation. We're sort of fifty-fifty in the operation. I look after New York and international distribution and she looks after the guns for drugs trade between Westland and across the border."

"Why did you choose Wiley Electronics?"

"We had been using another company, but

they went out of business, sort of like my husband did. For some reason the owner decided not to cooperate, and he mysteriously disappeared. Wiley Electronics just happened to be there when we needed it, and had all the connections, including international markets. Your computers are sold in almost every city in the world. We just removed the interior components, filled them with whatever was ordered, hid them in the middle of a shipment, and sent them off."

"Why the embezzlement?"

"That was Lennie Barnes' idiotic idea. He decided he could continue to pocket money from the deals he made for us, and also some extra from Wiley Electronics. He used his sister to help him. Same with the computers he was stealing. Most of them were outdated and nobody missed them, so he used them to start his own little drug trade."

"You let him get away with it?"

"For a while. We didn't know about the computers until recently. His sister talked too much when she was high. That's how we found out. We let Lennie take care of her. Then we took care of Lennie. He's around here somewhere. I believe he might be in one of those crushed vehicles over there."

"Why bomb George Brensley's car?"

"He knew too much."

"He didn't know anything, except for the embezzlement."

"Yes he did. Brensley knew there was money missing, and it was just a matter of time until he discovered where it was going, which would eventually lead to us. When Angelina overheard that you were returning to Westland to investigate, that clinched it. You both had to go, so we had Lennie plant a bomb in his car."

"Why the attempt to kill Lorraine and Jennifer on the highway?"

"Hatred. More of Barnes' idiotic ideas that brought attention to us."

"The bomb in New York? Was that your idea too?"

"No. I found out about it afterwards. They figured it was just a matter of time until you got suspicious, so they decided to kill you. Besides, they wanted control of your company."

"They? Who are, they?"

"My superiors. I don't see them very often, except once in a while when they come by with orders to be filled."

"What good would Wiley Electronics be to them if I'm dead?"

"Simple. You don't have any heirs. They didn't know who the business would go to, but it didn't really matter. They could keep your estate tied up for so many years with litigation that it wouldn't make much of a difference. And they could just go on using it the way they do now."

"How many contacts did you have in Wiley Electronics, besides Angelina?"

"No one. Didn't need them. Angelina has been with your company so long she knows where to find every nut and bolt, how to get to them, and how to get them out of the shipping department. Of course most of them went out in the form of drugs and guns and ammo."

"No one else?"

"No one else. We did invite some of your employees to parties and charitable functions at the estate, like Carl Rogers, John Wilson, and Paul Cater, but most of what we could learn in casual conversations we already knew."

Louise studied Jennifer. "You made a good choice Jim. She is a lot like me."

Jennifer glared back. "God, I hope not."

"It doesn't matter," Louise said. "You know we have to get rid of you, and Jim, and your friend, Lorraine. Please don't move."

"Don't move, yourself."

The order came from the direction of the building that Louise had left a few minutes before. She turned to see Jerry Whittnor and Charlie York walking out with their hands in the air. Behind them, his gun drawn, was George Brensley.

In the street they could hear sirens. Then several police cars raced through the junkyard and skidded to a stop around the building. Doors flung open and officers stood with guns pointed toward the group before them as they tried to sort out what was going on.

"Hold it," Lieutenant Lindsay called out as he approached, "I know these people."

"Who do we have here?" he asked.

"The two men are Jerry Whittnor and Charlie York," Jennifer replied. "They're in charge of the Westland portion of the guns for drugs trade."

"And the two ladies are Louise Fisher and Angelina Bales," Jim said. "They run the operation internationally and own Sandstorm Distribution."

"The Westland Police pulled the Sandstorm Distribution truck over a few blocks from here," Lindsay said. "It's the same one that was in your warehouse and was coming to pick up a shipment. But no Lennie Barnes."

Jim pointed to the crushed vehicles that Angelina had pointed out. "We've been told that Lennie is in one of those."

"And the drugs the Sandstorm truck was coming to pick up?" Lindsay asked as police officers frisked Louise, Angelina, and the two men who worked for them.

Louise didn't say anything. She didn't have to.

"In there," Jennifer said.

In a room at the back of the building, bundles were stacked. White powder flowed from a hole that had been made in one of them.

"It looks like you've just about wrapped things up here," Lindsay said. "I'll tidy up what's left and also get in touch with New York and have them look after Sandstorm there."

The lieutenant didn't ask for his accomplices' guns and they didn't volunteer to provide them. "I have to say, it's been an experience being part of your gang," he said with a positive grin.

"For us too," Jennifer said as she looked around the yard and whistled for Sheeba.

Snuggled beside the heroic border collie, not looking anything like the ferocious dog they had encountered earlier, was Brutus.

TWENTY-TWO

To others in the city, there might have been action and excitement and problems to solve, but to Jim and Jennifer and George and Lorraine, Westland seemed very quiet.

Louise Fisher, Angelina Bales, Jerry Whittnor and Charlie York, along with other members of the crime family were in custody, and the guns for drug trade, or at least the Westland-East Coast connection, had been broken up.

Lennie Barnes was dead. His life was over when the family learned he was using their Mercedes limo and Sandstorm Distribution truck for his unauthorized late night embezzlements, computer thefts, drug trades, and assassination attempts.

The junkyard could look forward to a happier future. An anonymous donor, who was no longer losing money from embezzlement and having his company's shipping department used for drug and weapon transactions, decided to buy it, clean it up, and turn it over to the city for a park. The area was to be dedicated to the fondly remembered old couple who had once owned it and welcomed in kids to find parts for their bicycles.

"Why would Louise Fisher help you in New York and lead you right to the Sandstorm warehouse?" Lorraine asked.

"She knew I was going to find out about the Sandstorm truck anyway," Jim replied. "I was on my way to the shipping department to ask if they had ever heard of it. She just decided to help me find something I was going to eventually discover anyway. She went with me to the Sandstorm warehouse for the same reason, to keep an eye on me. She helped me break in because she knew I was going to get in one way or another."

"Didn't the man there recognize her?"

"No, and she was genuinely frightened. She thought he was going to shoot both of us. The phone call he was making when we made our escape was to Angelina Bales to ask who we were. When I left Louise, she also called Angelina with instructions to tell Whittnor and York to get rid of the shipment of drugs that was at the junkyard, then she took her private jet to Westland. Too bad. In her hurry to let her sister-in-law know about what was going on, she used her own phone, and the New York police traced both calls."

"Are they going to recover any of the money that Lennie Barnes was embezzling from Wiley Electronics?" Lorraine asked.

"Probably not, but at least we shouldn't lose any more, unless there's another Angelina lurking somewhere in the company. She was Louise's eyes and ears. When we saw Lennie drive by Wiley Electronics on his way to the junkyard, he was supposed to contact Angelina and find out if anyone would be working late and if the shipping department would be clear for the drugs and weapons trade."

"What were Wiley Electronics employees doing at the Charity Event?"

"Just that. They were invited, like a lot of other people, to support a charity and help out the community. They didn't know Whittnor liked to engage donors in conversation to pick up bits of information he could use."

"And the airport car rental clerk that George thought was mixed up with the bombing of his Buick?"

"The only thing he did was accidentally set off the bomb. But he was an important connection that helped lead us to the crime family and the drugs for guns trade."

"Lieutenant Raymond Lindsay of the Westland Police Department? How is he doing?"

"Lieutenant Lindsay is no longer in the employ of the Westland Police Department."

"Retired," George asked.

"Semi," Jim replied. "Harry Haddel, the senior partner in a local private investigation company has decided to also semi-retire, and the lieutenant was offered a partnership in the firm. According to Jennifer, she will still be a moll, except with two different partners."

"You still have a problem with management in your company," George reminded him. "Carl Rogers is a good man, but he's in the wrong position."

"I know," Jim said. "So does Carl. He talked to me. He said he wanted to give up his job as regional manager and go back to what he does best and loves, selling. I asked him if he would consider taking over international sales and marketing, and he jumped at it. He'll be doing everything that Louise was doing, except instead of buying computers and having Sandstorm fill them full of drugs for shipment around the world, he'll be selling to them direct from Wiley Electronics."

"Who are you going to get to replace him?" Lorraine asked.

"I've already chosen a replacement. I've decided to take the job myself. I've also decided to relocate Wiley Electronics International Headquarters to Westland."

The others looked at him and smiled. Their agreement showed on their faces.

"What about your other manufacturing plants around the world? Who's going to manage them?"

"Our New York manager, Joanne Kent. She already looks after much of the international end of the business, and enjoys the travel. But I'll still be doing some."

"Is there any particular reason you decided to come back to Westland?"

"Yes. As much as I enjoy traveling around the world, this is my home. But there are other reasons too."

George and Lorraine smiled at each other. "I told you it would work," Lorraine said.

"What would work?" Jennifer asked, trying not to appear that she knew what Lorraine was talking about.

"Oh, just a little matchmaking," George said. "Lorraine thought you two might hit it off. But that wasn't the only reason she introduced Jim to you. You're still the best private investigator we know."

"I'm the only private investigator you know," Jennifer laughed.

"She's the best one I know too," Jim said, putting his arms around her.

"Isn't it funny," Jennifer said. "You look for someone all your life and then one day he just walks into your office because his company is being stolen from under him by embezzlers and international crime."

"Or junkyards," George added, gesturing toward the two dogs that had wandered in from the yard.

"It was nice of you to give Brutus a home," Lorraine said to Jennifer.

"It was the least I could do," she replied. "If he hadn't fallen for Sheeba and let you three into the junkyard, I don't know where I'd be."

"Love is wonderful," Lorraine sighed as she embracing her husband and watched the two dogs snuggling together across the room.

"It sure is," Jennifer agreed, putting her arms around Jim.

"It sure is," Jim replied, hugging her back.

It was good to be back in Westland.

acadiascale.com

Acadia Scale Press books
may be purchased at
amazon.com
barnes&noble.com

Stores, gift shops, and libraries
may order our books through

INGRAM BOOK COMPANY
and
BAKER & TAYLOR BOOKS